© Dis Voir, 2007

1 Cité Riverin

F - 75010 Paris

http://www.disvoir.com

ISBN : 9782914563314

PRINTED IN EUROPE

THE HISTORIANS

BOOK 39

ALSO PUBLISHED BY DIS VOIR

PETER GREENAWAY

series "cinema-fiction"

Gold
The Falls
Rosa
Fear of Drowning by numbers

series "cinema/ script"
Nightwatching
The cook, the thief, his wife and her lover
The baby of mâcon
The belly of an architect
A zed and two noughts
Eight and a half women
The pillow book
Drowning by numbers

PETER GREENAWAY

THE HISTORIANS
BOOK 39
THE RISE & FALL OF
GESTURES DRAMA

1. A flagging motion performed without any attempt to beg a lift.
The gesture was witnessed by travellers at the Rowley Crossroads. The flagger was considered to be a mild nuisance at best, and as a harmless madman at worst. His daily occupation was unknown. Some said he was a vagrant. Nobody at the time regarded him as a self-conscious performer, though later historians of Gestures Theatre made him significant; they referred to him first of all as the Rowley Crossroads Performer, and then simply as Rowley. They made him a hero.

2. Two bird catchers standing on a podium in Dissart made flapping gestures.
It has been suggested that these gestures were made to advertise what the bird-catchers had to sell. They made profits in excess of their expectations. Correlations of strict material gain and aesthetic enjoyment were idly calculated, and it was decided that, in these particular circumstances, both characteristics could be considered as equal.

3. Gentle gestures of bowing and then the pressing together of hands were made at Germander.
These gestures were seen in the porch of the Germander Outdoor-Speaking-House on a Spring evening when the strolling crowds were returning home from a race-meeting. The initial gestures were made, it seemed, to express sheer delight without any profit to be gained by either the satisfaction of expressing social comment or of merchandising. It had, after all, always readily been understood in Germander that there were other and better currencies than irony or money.
This incident stands as the first recorded occasion of a company self-consciously concerned to make a show before an audience by the exhibition of gestures for mutual gratification. Their activity certainly promoted thought about the disinterested gesture, the gesture indeed

[8]   made for its own sake. It was seriously proposed that no action could be conceived that did not seek a reward, any reward, even a smile.

4. A flapping motion made by two silent orators.

The orators were accompanied by a white terrier dog. The event was witnessed for seven minutes on an empty set of stone steps at the Throatan'blade Customs House. It was understood that the intention was to express a metaphor by gesture, and the metaphor was interpreted by some to be an indication of new winds coming from contrary directions. There were various attempts to justify the dog, saying it was a floating punctuation mark in the proceedings, or a deliberately introduced distraction, or a jocular ingredient to lighten the polemic, or indeed a veiled blasphemy since dog spelt backwards always spells god. Some said the dog was prophetic and would one day give a significant signal, all that was necessary was to wait for it to bark at just the right moment in just the right circumstances. Opinions settled down to agree that the canine, universal symbol both of lechery and faithfulness, which somehow sounds contradictory, was ultimately to be recognised as the necessary licensed jester in the piece. Members of the audience less prone to strive to seek a meaning believed the dog was simply entertaining itself, a dog being simply a dog. Perhaps it was attracted by the closeness of the sympathetic and friendly crowd, though to contemporary ears this observation could sound like sentimental anthropomorphism. Whatever the interpretation, and to help explain the considerable labouring to understand a meaning for its presence, it is certain that this is the first recorded instance of a dog in Gestures Drama. In one guise or another, the dog was to stay.

The pair of Throatan'blade performers were to be known as *The First Dog Twin Players*, and, in later years, it was considered prophetic that their occupation was listed as oratory, which is nothing if not an occupation relevant to expressing ideas through the voice, and here was an event where the voice was to be strenuously denied.

5. Two men dressed in white hats, white baggy trousers and white buttoned [9]
jackets performed gestures on the scaffolding boards outside a baker's shop in
Hawsterly.

The men gestured with wide sweeping arms, curled fingers and
dancing legs. Any suggestion that they were costumed as bakers and
were advertising buns was unlikely, for the baker repeatedly chased
them away. This performance could be said to be the first time
Gestures Drama was accompanied with ritualised dressing-up.

6. A woman and three men gestured with much portentousness to suggest the
Passing of History. With a waving and scooping motion they encouraged
History to pass on by. Sometimes slow, sometimes fast, sometimes diffidently.
History for them never stopped moving.
They swooped and scooped, flagged and waved, sometimes with the
outstretched arm, sometimes with the hand, sometimes just with the index
finger of the right hand.

The performers were dressed in yellow furred gowns that were old
enough to have been fashionable in the years of their grandparents,
and brought to mind polar bears soaked in urine. The fact that the
performance happened far to the North suggests that the activities
of Gestures Drama were spreading, and that costuming was
confirmed as being relevant to the experience, though cynical
detractors suggested the furred gowns were worn simply to keep
the participants from freezing to death. This is the first recorded
incident of female participation in Gestures Drama.
It was noted at the time that the very first activities of Gestures
Drama were associated primarily with the arms and consisted in
flagging and flapping motions, the elementary vocabulary of both
fright and flight.

7. A repeated turn of the head towards the source of an innocent sound by a young
man dressed in silver paper that seemed to be stuck to his naked body with spittle.
This repeated gesture was considered significant by those in future
years researching the introduction of sound in Gestures Drama. It

[10] must be stressed that the young man himself did not make any sound whatsoever.

The *"Innocent Sound"* has been investigated as a reoccurring phenomenon. In this instance the sound is reported to have come from the empty field across from the Ladderheigh Resting-Place that many called The Tile-ling or the Tile-Field, the site of a tile factory that later had been turned into a palace-garden which subsequently had been destroyed. The essence of an *"Innocent Sound"* originating in an empty field opposite a Gestures Drama Theatre has since assumed a significance in the whole phenomenon of Gestures Drama. It laid down the beginnings of a mythology concerning the origins of Gestures vocalisation, though the phenomenon and its attendant mythologies may have been created as a strategy to ensure that no single person could be blamed for the advent of sound in the genre, since, certainly initially, vocalisation in Gestures Drama was a shocking, unpopular and unwelcome affair, bringing opprobrium on all who suggested its possible existence.

8. A gesture of the constant turning of the head by a young woman dressed in a red wig and with a red-painted face, was reported at the Fadderlay Evening Market-Place. The action was accompanied by a rhythmic and simultaneous flexing of the knees.

Beyond the concentrated ambition of wishing to strongly demonstrate a facial profile to her audience, the implications of the woman's gesturing were debatable, but archivists make this event the first recorded instance of the use of wigs, cosmetics and the exploitation of a popular gathering place to find an audience. Considering the location and the time of day, detractors of Gestures Theatre infer that this is an example of the genre simply following money, and that the performer was a woman of easy virtue drawing attention to herself.

9. On Tivermeat Pier on the River Acrow, a company of seven costumed men walking on boards strung across the water offered seats to an audience that they might watch silent gestures of joy in some comfort for fourteen minutes.

This is the first occurrence of a direct regard for audience convenience. The performers wore yellow-painted wooden shoes. Any suggestion that the wooden shoes were used for sound punctuation must be considered to be a hindsight consideration made by those seeking to find the advent of conscious sound in Gestures Drama, but it is true that clogs were subsequently to be seen frequently on a Gestures Drama stage.

10. A certain flicking and flexing of the whole body in irritation as though the performer was simulating the characteristics of a horse annoyed by flies.
The performer had a shaved head and wore a tight-fitting costume of wet white silk that gave his body an equine sheen. His movements started at the head and moved through the body to the buttocks where, since a human has no tail, the gestures were accomplished with some extra and very applaudable panache. One implication of the performance was surely to indicate that horses are naked, and when a man rides a horse he is riding a naked animal. Some suggested the total body gesture was metaphorical propaganda for a communal migration away from a source of irritation, and many commentators turned their attention to identify the significance of the flies. Much was made of the actor's buttocks, but his total guilelessness protected him from exploitation. He managed to retain his innocence, a situation which in turn enflamed a greater desire to see him perform. The gesturer's name was Accreditor and on the occasion of this performance he was seventeen. As a precise perfectionist, he was to draw very large admiring crowds at all his subsequent performances in many different characterisations, though he was to perform rarely, maybe only once or twice a year.

11. A kicking motion performed after dark by candle-light at Hooden 'badly.
This was the first example of night-time Gestures Drama Entertainment.

[12]

12. Seven numbered gestures performed by an elderly woman dressed in a pale blue muslin skirt marked with a purple cuneiform pattern.

The skirt decoration made the woman look as though she laboured in the shade of a blossoming plumbago tree on a summer evening. The purpose of her activities appeared to indicate how to lay a crisp white sheet on a bed intended for lovers in three and a half minutes. The flying white sheet rose up in the air seven times accompanied by the woman holding up the requisite number of fingers each time. The audience was certainly made to understand that the number seven was to be considered as significant. Perhaps the number seven was to be regarded as a symbolic calculation to attract fecundity, after all, the seventh wave, the seventh day, the seventh son, the seventh dream, were all considered to be larger or more powerful or more significant than their six predecessors. This performance, created with intense attention to small detail, is representative of many such performances now appearing in the West and South-West that demonstrated an increasing use of more intimate subject-matter, an acknowledgement of the domestic, a political concern for the female and some emphasis on the superstitious.

13. A silent gesture recorded in a temporary Gestures Theatre Space at Hailbellow to demonstrate a dressed woman blown by a strong wind from the South.

14. A silent gesture recorded in a second Gestures Theatre Space at Hailbellow to indicate an undressed woman blown by a strong wind from the South.

There was an immediate outcry because of the display of nudity. The accusation of exhibitionism may not have been unreasonable, but the objections could have been better justified if the audience had understood that the undressed woman was making a bid to primarily shamelessly celebrate and triumphantly exhibit her expertise and virtuosity, and not essentially her body. After all, it is far more difficult to convince an audience that a cold wind was blowing whilst not wearing clothes, than with. This gestures

actress was twenty-three and her Gestures Drama stage-name was [13]
Bithet. She was later infamously known as the Gestures Bitch.

15. In the Washing-Place at Poure Aspect, in the West of the country, a silent gesture was performed that was entirely pleasurable and made to suggest that the colour red was positive and beneficial.

The gesture was performed by three women who began the performance wearing crimson feathered hats with stiff broad brims that shaded their eyes in a warm red glow. The audience apparently had no difficulty whatsoever in understanding that what was being performed was indeed a positive reaction to the colour red. Performances like this began to demonstrate the capacity to consider abstract concepts as being very suitable material for Gestures Drama.

16. In the Drying Tower at Poure Distract, four bare-breasted women performed gestures that were intended to indicate that the colour red was hostile and malevolent.

This gesture was intended to be inimical to the activities performed in the Washing-Place in Poure South, evidence of Gesture Drama performers becoming aware of themselves as proponents of social argument. This is an early example of a Gestures Theatre of Responses where a performer or company set up a performance that needed to be answered by another performer or company to make indeed a genre of theatrical conversation. In some instances this activity became complex when a third, a fourth and even a fifth actor or company continued the dialogue, provoking indeed, if the public continued to be fascinated, the first actor or company to restate their proposition. After the third performance at the Drying Tower, the women were encouraged to conceal their breasts, and they did so by wearing papier-mâché brassieres, moulded from their own bodies but one size larger, and taking advantage of the situation, they painted the nipples a paler pink that the originals.

[14]   *17. The first official mention of the term "Gesturer" as an occupation description was used in a thirty-five minute performance piece at Gopplar, where a patrician middle-aged man made gestures to indicate his grief for the proletariat victims of a flood.*

A word previously used for a gesture performer was simply "player", or indeed "performer", but it was too vague and could have referred to participants in other genres of dramatic performance. In this instance, the gesturer attempted an identification with the victims he grieved over by wearing unbleached underlinen whilst standing in a blue porcelain basin that was full of water and broken mirrors that reflected flickering light up onto his body.

18. A twenty-one minute gestures dance to express injustices through the Passage of History. The hands were never lowered beneath the shoulders.

19. The smallest throw-away gesture possible to show a desire for death, suggesting extreme stoicism, but a stoicism way beyond any personal vanity.

20. A gesture made to demonstrate the mixed signals sent by a suicide.

21. A gesture made to suggest an abhorrence of flight.

22. The first purpose-built Gestures Drama Theatre premiered a work that featured almost exclusively the activities of a fat man wishing to be thin.

The theatre was constructed of blue-ink-stained wood with a stage to be viewed from three sides erected at the eye-level of a seated adult. On the fourth side of the stage was a garden of seven ilex trees. A bush of a thousand blooms growing in an unglazed earthenware pot was placed on a discrete flat wooden platform on almost entirely concealed wheels. The trees in the garden were rooted and immovable; occasionally their dark tapering tops bent and waved in a controlled breeze. The potted bush on the stage was movable.

The performance was variously tragic and comic, forever wrong-footing the expectations of the audience. The major performer Optocol astonished everyone by his ingenuity of convincing the audience of being twenty stone at the start of the performance and only eight stone at its finish. As if to demonstrate the loss of twelve stone, a pile of steaming faeces accumulated on a large blue porcelain tray placed on the left of the stage. A small bare-footed boy in a red gown repeatedly entered the stage to deposit the faeces and water the bush until it did indeed blossom with a thousand blooms to accompany and parallel the fat man's increasing delight at becoming thin. This sort of transformation and gradual metamorphosis became Optocol's identifiable performance characteristic. On later memorable occasions he would start a performance as a corpse and end it as an embryo, or begin as a man writing his name in the snow with the stream of his urine, and finish it as a woman expelling milk from both breasts.

23. *A twenty-eight minute gesture of grief by a man burying his wife.*
The actor, Apt Cleaf, performed on a solid six foot cube-block of wood hewn from the bole of a cork oak that had been blackened by fire and then oiled. He used three spades, one of gold, one of silver and one of lead. The impossibility of burying a corpse in a solid block of hard wood heightened the frustrations and anger caused by death and loss. The performance became a blue-print of how to express great grief at the loss of a loved one by demonstrating that grief is a form of angry frustration that cannot in the end be negotiated, only endured.

24. *An adroit and persistent turning to the left to avoid an accident with a stampeding animal.*
The two accomplished performers of this drama acted in a perfectly synchronous movement, and the invisible panicking animal constantly changed its identity. Such was the skill of the performers that the audience, behaving as a single unit, became afraid of an animal attack, but were never certain whether it was to come from in front or from behind, from the air, or, indeed, from under the ground. Every evening more than a few audience members, overcome by anxiety, left their seats and had to be escorted home. One scared

[16] young woman asked the theatre attendant accompanying her to search under her bed and look in all her cupboards. She persuaded him to hold her hand when she fell asleep. Nine months later they became the parents of a left-handed child.

An elderly man taken home in a hand-cart was found dead the next day. He was seated in his bath with a fierce look of horror frozen on his face. His head, turned to the left, was fixed in rigour mortis, and the wounds of a horned animal scarred his chest and abdomen.

25. A gesture that indicates the reluctant preparation for a triumph.
It was the first recorded use of real and not imagined animals, apart from dogs, on the Gestures Drama stage. The Gestures Player employed two ostriches to represent exotic animal booty.

26. A silent gesture constantly repeated, reconciling a small fiction to a large truth too many times to make it believable.
The performance in a dilapidated theatre was enthusiastically applauded by twenty members of a financial establishment who offered to fund the theatre's refurbishment and encourage the burgeoning growth of *"The Habit of the Lie"*.

27. A gesture by three performers that demonstrated the irritation of relating a tedious dream to an audience for a second time. The performers were dressed as crowned kings and each was accompanied by a costumed dog that barked on demand.
The members of the audience were at first flattered by being made aware that they were part of the drama, but then felt insulted because the three kings made it clear that they considered the audience too stupid to be presented with an intelligent performance. This aggressive performer and audience relationship became a feature of Southern Gestures Drama and was eventually to develop in very disturbing ways. An audience's sense of its own collective masochism and its willingness to accept the role of a victim was essential to make such drama viable.

28. *A series of forty-nine gestures that demonstrated the reconstruction of* [17]
anything from a roof to a marriage.

29. *A Counting Gestures Drama.*
The first true playbill for a silent Gesturing Theatre performance
was displayed in Matteridgean'then. Sixty by ninety centimetres, it
was printed on a coarse white paper in a dark blue ink. The text ran:

A Theatre of Gestures Drama
Performing Counting and Demarcating Silent Gestures
With a Mathematician, An Arithmetician and a Simple Counter.
To be solicitously performed
On the Slope, Matteridgean'then

This may very well be the first time the phrase "*A Theatre of Gestures*"
had been committed to a written text. It must be said that the three
performers responsible also used texts on the stage written with chalk
on portable blackboards, thus creating a direct correspondence between
the calculated use of text on stage and the use of text in the playbill.
After two further productions, this Matteridgean'then Company
ceased performing. Two of their members set up a publishing
company specialising in servicing the new cultural phenomenon
sometime known as "*The Lying-In*", or "*The Habit of the Lie*". It was
noted that management, performers and audience responded posi-
tively to the addition of written text to Gestures Drama. Undoubtedly extra meaning could be communicated by the addition of text,
though purists for silent Gestures Drama deplored its introduction
and lobbied for its removal.

30. *The first Gestures Drama Primer.*
Perhaps enheartened by the use of text at Matteridgean'then, a
young Selfsettle lawyer, Edweiss, devised a textual way to record
the vocabulary of Gestures Theatre. His system divided the body
into thirty-five numbered sections, permitting each section seven
individual movements. He indicated the direction of each gesture
by arrows, the speed of each gesture by numbers in a rising scale of

[18] ten, and the strength of each gesture by the letters A to M, A being very weak, and M being very strong. He published a book of tables and diagrams, and to introduce it to a potential public, at his own expense, he rented a schoolroom in the Scholastic House in Biccastria, and employed a young man from the Gestchoker Gestures Company to demonstrate the itemised 259 movements. He paid an experienced draughtsman to draw every itemised gesture of the young man as he stood naked on a table in a haze of chalk dust, trying to stay awake, his body arranged in its fixed positions by an exacting and very impatient Edweiss. Starting around midday, the whole activity took over twelve hours, and continued by candle-light until well after midnight. The original drawings were subsequently valued and treasured, but the book of texts, diagrams and engravings did not sell well. It was probably too early for such a venture, general audiences being not yet fascinated enough in Gestures Drama to engage in such refined observations.

31. A series of silent gestures to show a deaf man finding his hearing by increasing degrees.
This gestures performance was advertised as a deliberate attempt to process Time, but many saw it as a start to a subversive attempt to introduce sound into Gestures Drama.

32. A silent Gestures Drama to show that the main protagonist in the piece, who we might very well refer to as the hero, believed in the axiom that the criminal was always ahead of the police.
However, the main protagonist cited one aberration when the police appeared to be ahead of the criminal, when an arresting marshal jailed a woman for soliciting the use of her body before she had actually done so. This was again an attempt to interfere with Time, but essentially it caught the public's attention because such was the quality of the performance, members of the audience were convinced that they had seen the woman exhibiting her breasts and lifting her dress, and when

questioned, gave detailed and provable evidence of what they had seen as to the woman's rouged nipples and shaven pudenda. It was said that the Gestures actress was Bithet, known as the Gestures' Bitch. She was now thirty-one.

33. A silent gesture to show that a man enjoyed the taste of blood.
The activity was considered inappropriate because the player was performing at a celebration associated with a naming ceremony. He was sent away from the private party with a bruised face and a sack of beans. The former was a punishment for his effrontery, the latter, his payment. This sort of Gestures Drama was generally misunderstood, which was part of the intention. It was called *Utochic Gestures Drama*, after its originator, Benavo Utochi, who had come from the South. He was determined to move Gestures Drama away from any taint of bourgeois appropriation as a vehicle for consolation. Most Utochi performers considered the body as an automaton to be used as the scaffolding for gesture. They often treated human anatomy with contempt. It was mere machinery, an assemblage of spare parts, and they did not care if the body was bruised, scratched, knocked, scarred or wounded in performance. To accentuate the appearance of an automaton, some performers tied waxed string tightly around the body, at the top of the arms, the top of the legs, around the midriff and the neck, and around the ankles and wrists, to indicate the segmented characteristics of the body and imply that the body might be disassembled at these junctures and be re-assembled with other parts, as was in the nature of certain manufactured life-sized wooden dolls currently available in the whore-houses of PastonCumber.

34. A paralysed victim of a gravity accident made the customary gestures in performance of a bald man pretending to have hair.
The pathos of the man's atrophied legs drew sympathy, but the fact that the absent hair was growing, or rather not growing, on his belly, excited derision and antipathy. This was another example of Utochic Gestures Drama.

[20]   *35. Apparently paid handsomely to perform, a 25 year old female virgin silently practised the gestures of sexual experience in front of a mirror.*
The audience were only allowed to see the reflection of the gestures performer and not the performer. A prosecution of the commissioning patrons was promised, but it is believed compound bribery associated with blackmail created circumstances that caused the case to be dismissed. The woman is now married to the Marshal Promost who prizes the woman's virginity. His physical contact with his wife goes no further than to occasionally and gently breathe on the glass that reflects her nakedness.

36. A faint gesture to imply an elderly man was pretending to be unaffected by a very painful rejection of love.
Benavo Utochi himself played the elderly man, squatting on his haunches, tracing with his right index finger the words *"my heart"*, in a puddle of his own lukewarm urine.

37. Utochi committed public suicide as an ultimate gesture of personal negligence and neglect, and he was buried in a horse trough filled with quick-lime.
In Utochi's honour, a performance by nine of his acolytes was advertised, but then banned for anticipated moral turpitude. In protest the nine players stood stock still on the Grasminder stage dressed in white shifts buttoned up to the neck to symbolically keep in all transgressions. They had halters around their shoulders and their feet were tied together with ivy. They were applauded for an hour by over six hundred enthusiastic Utochi supporters. The audience probably imagined the banned indignities to be more disturbing than the actors had ever intended, prompting the cultural commentator Simploner to state that this event must surely be the greatest success Gestures Drama was capable of, for this enthusiastic, exuberant audience was applauding the product of its own imagination. The audience afterwards refused to leave the theatre. They disinterred Utochi's lime-corroded corpse and set

it up in the Oketub-Bey Marketplace, beside an effigy of Rowley, [21] the mythical founder of their profession who had flagged as a gesture at the Rowley Crossroads in the already almost legendary past of Gestures Drama.

38. A silent gesture by an actress playing an old woman to suggest contempt for a disagreeable opinion in a book written at the time of her father's youth.

It was not easy to differentiate between the actor's intentions and the character's intentions. The actress's name was Pollity Bellor. She was to make, in her long career in the theatre, a Gestures study of ageing, demonstrating both its gradual but dignified onslaught, and also the attempts of vanity to keep it at bay. On her fiftieth birthday, after 32 years of Gestures Drama, she knew that she had tried hard and long enough within the confines of her chosen subject to feel she had no more to contribute, and she retired into a cushioned obscurity organised by her lovers. Many admirers sought her out and made totally unprovable claims that she was still working, but in deep disguise. She was last definitively seen swimming in a river near Acceptivia. She was wearing a tight-fitting bathing cap that hid her greying hair.

39. A register was started at Jatchett that officially noted Gestures Theatre Performance titles with their associated casts, managers and playhouse names.

It was a first tentative attempt to defend Gestures Drama against plagiarism, though the register could not enforce any copyright. Any protection was affected only through the possibility of engendering shame among those who were caught stealing material. The register stationery was printed with a male figure drawn in the attitude of gesturing shame, that had been borrowed without permission from the Matteridgean'then book of Gestures Drama Movements by Edweiss.

However, since texts were only just beginning to be used in Gestures Theatre, and there was still comparatively little

[22]   standardisation among descriptions, ambiguity was prevalent and claims of originality were difficult to substantiate. Players who moved from one company to another often took material with them, with, as often as not, a real claim to own it. Mappito, the dog-mime, for example, was notorious for doing this, but such was his popularity, he always managed to remain unpenalized.

40. The first suggestion of Gestures Drama being self-consciously subversive as regards the subject of nudity was promulgated after thirty-five years of recognised practice.

The objections curiously seemed more to do with effrontery to legislation than any display of anatomical parts normally kept concealed. Encouraged by the success of being able to offend bureaucracy, small Gestures Theatre Companies along the Uraguar valley presented audiences with stripping shows, though the audiences were not necessarily encouraged to see them like that. Their programme, subsequently copied, was advertised as *The Small and The Great Unclothings*. Critical of audience voyeurism, other companies *"stripped"* whilst staying fully dressed, developing a vocabulary that, it was said, became extremely sophisticated and very erotic, without necessarily attracting adverse censorship. Such activities encouraged discussion of whether or not there should be a form of external censorship, or that, at the very least, strong pressure should be brought to encourage self-censorship. This is the very first time that veiled talk of the idea of Theatre Police was instigated.

41. The first attempt at a serious critical review of a Gestures Theatre performance was by a history academician, Uritano Croquer.

Croquer was a collector of painted figurative images, and a painfully thin man with a skin complaint that badly disfigured his body. He was reputed to have been both the nephew and the reluctant lover of Pollity Bellor, for which incestuous activity, it is said, he had been inflicted with his disfiguring disease. He saw important connections between current painted images and the activities of what he witnessed on stage in the towns of the Centre Edge. He concentrated on discussing, with some considerable thoroughness, a successful Gestures Theatre performance called *"Understanding from Here to There"*, played by a company of seven players with an event structured on the Seven Ages of Man, where the overall ambience was optimistic and celebratory. It was a good choice of public drama on which to write a serious and painstaking review since the performance was a quality piece and had been seen by a large audience, thus stimulating considerable enquiry and debate. An interesting problem arose at once as to find a good vocabulary to make references to what was happening on stage, for the performance, to give it any justice, required long descriptions of its visual gestures, which were often of some complexity, and it was quickly realised that the very characteristic uniqueness of these gestures and their usages were essentially non-translatable in any other genre, true proof that Gestures Drama had come of age and could be truly regarded as an autonomous instrument. The review, by its very obvious inadequacies of communication - to do not with the author's inabilities, but to do with the paucity of necessary language - emphasised some of the essences of Gestures Theatre, and set up large curiosities in audiences wishing to see the performance for themselves.

The review, undoubtedly widely read, caused some consternation, such that there was a pause of some months before valuable reaction and response set in and the consequences digested. Maybe it took that amount of time for other commentators to gather together their critical apparatus, and indeed their courage, to commit their thoughts to print. When they did publish, and all in a sudden rush, the ensuing publicity created a credibility for Gestures Drama that was never subsequently questioned. The silence of silent Gestures Drama was perceived as a necessity. To interfere with that characteristic was, according to the cultural commentator Croquer, a heresy, bound to dilute the hard-won language of a profound new means of expression that could be said to have truly arrived.

[24]   In a larger community of some estimated sixty million inhabitants speaking some two hundred languages, and many more dialects, a non-vocal theatrical communication vehicle seemed desirable, if not simply for its own sake, then as a binding community phenomenon to be used by the well-meaning to build cohesion. The unscrupulous of course also perceived the advantages. It was well within the vested interests of the malevolent to preserve the status quo, and keep Gestures Drama a silent phenomenon uncontaminated by the differences of language.

42. *A company at Denderon attracted attention by a Standing Gestures performance of great expertise. They expressed mass and weight, some trusting and some not trusting the floor of the stage, and some liking and some not liking the floor of the stage.*

The company were making a comment perhaps on the desire to feel secure enough to live permanently in metaphorical towers high above the ground, and also to imagine if the texture of the sea in fact should be as it was commonly imagined to be. The contentious volume *"To the Ocean"* had recently been published in PastonCumber and was already creating waves of delight, dispute and dissension. It is certain that the Denderon Company elaborated and extended the debate.

43. *Two companies of Gesture Players pooled their resources at Gneiper, and erected a painted wooden statue of Rowley, the mythical founder of Gestures Drama.*

The statue was placed at the centre rear of the wooden platform stage, where it became variously a butt for amusement or an altar for genuflexion, or was treated as the symbol of a minor deity who had to be appeased. Subsequently, by frequent public familiarity, this stage became known as the Rowley Theatre.

No-one could know what the almost legendary Rowley looked like, and the wood-carver gave him a long nose, large hooded eyes and tightly closed lips, no doubt reacting to received opinions of how a founder of Silent Gestures Theatre should appear. This image, certainly in profile, became a fixture. Its salient characteristics appeared in playbills. Constantly copied and re-copied, the [25] distinguishing features became exaggerated. The nose grew longer and the lips became so reduced they almost ceased to exist. At Raggerdowning, with a bust made of black polished lead, the lips disappeared altogether, perhaps as a result of the particular wish of the theatre proprietor who was adamant to the point of extreme aggression against any form of vocalisation in Gestures Drama.

Rowley Playhouses appeared in the South so frequently that theatres became known as Rowleys or rowelies, the word no longer spelt with a capital letter. In the towns of the Knipperlin, rowelies were constructed in many marketplaces with the effigy of Rowley becoming a main feature of the stage architecture, erected like the decorated prow figurehead of a river-ship, garlanded on holidays, dressed in coloured furs in winter, disfigured by iconoclasts, scribbled with graffiti and given a pink and black phallus every Spring by the lascivious. A Rowley statue was made female in Joggernost, had its ears knocked of in Parfley, and was burnt down in Jickering. In Hadderplea, the Rowley effigy became a petitioning post for the lambjammers who hammered up their grievances on its stocky torso. Frequent theatre-goers, who could often gesturally reproduce some seventy minutes of a performance in detail from memory, were nicknamed the *"long noses"*, on account of Rowley's long nose. The popular Gerfleet Menagerie at Kertuffey with its exhibition of elephants was opened in association with a Gestures Drama performance. The elephants were regarded with great attention and affection, and immediately gained a reputation as being amorous animals with long penises, long memories and long noses. Commentators, putting elephants and Gesture Drama presentation together, began to call persistent Gesture Drama theatre-goers *" the theatre elephants"*. A play registered at the Jatchett Repository was called The Elephant Rowlies, creating an etymological puzzle of considerable mystery for foreign philologists. When the new playhouse was built at Yalt, the Wowelly, as it was called in dialect, for the local community affected a lisp, Rowley's effigy was fashioned with the head and trunk of an elephant, and a lampooning nursery rhyme became familiar.

> *Laugh, laugh, the crows do cry,*
> *The elephants are coming to drown,*
> *Some with dogs and some in clogs,*
> *Rowley's flagging his clown.*

A crow was a local name for a whore. Women of easy virtue invariably wore untidy black wigs and were commonly considered to be noisy, raucous and greedy. Collectively soliciting outside the theatres, these ladies of the night had been moved to derisory laughter over the prospect of Gestures Drama enthusiasts hurrying to immerse themselves, with their absurd wooden footwear, in the copious semen, real and metaphorical, of Gestures Drama. Flagging, because of the repetitious hand movements, was a euphemism for masturbating. A clown was a penis, because of its absurd appearance, its bulbous hat, and its laughable antics, and Rowley became a stud or a catamite depending upon the commentator's enthusiasms for the art of Gestures Theatre.

44. A complicated movement made in an attempt to find a new way to express intense carnal love from the female point of view.
This was considered to be an exhibitionist gesture originating from a desire to be novel for its own sake. It also implied, even to the sophisticated, an unusual sexual anatomy.

45. A gesture of praise from a blind deaf-mute.
This gesture was considered illogical, but its unfathomable meaning generated a small genre of Gestures Drama Performances that had a following for those who enjoyed intractable puzzles or else delighted in carefully crafted self-conscious absurdity.

46. It was at Denderon where the theatrical possibilities of the contentious volume of sea-exploration, "To the Ocean", were first exploited, that the concept of the Steady-State Player was first remarked upon.

There may or may not be a connection between these two facts, but it [27] cannot go entirely unnoticed that blue was the colour, supposedly, of the sea and certainly also of this ground-breaking individual.

Gestures Drama had developed sufficient excitement to attract fanatics, but there were many such people who could not really make any contribution to the phenomenon that they might enjoy to the full, or make sufficiently manifest, to satisfy their desire to be involved. Many of these theatre admirers would admit to the fascination of wishing to be watched like an actor is watched, but had no talent or aptitude for being a performer.

It was said that the first acknowledged Steady-State Performer, an elderly woman known as the Blue Widow, was wealthy enough to be able to pay the theatre manager at Denderon to permit her to sit on the edge of the stage on a low stool under a parasol. She would watch the drama for the first seven minutes like everyone else, and then she turned the stool around so that she watched the audience, or rather the audience watched her. She did not do anything at all, beyond occasionally wiping the end of her nose with a blue handkerchief - hence her nickname. She wore a different blue-accessorised dress for each new play, a dress that had been decided upon after she had attended the play's rehearsals, and after she had studied the drama's gestures, content and mis-en-scène.

Eventually the Blue Widow had plucked up courage to ask, and, of course, to pay, the wardrobe mistress to permit her to wear a costume from the theatre wardrobe, a costume suitable for the play in question. Eventually the theatre management agreed to design the woman a costume of her own, a useful idea because her appearance could, in this way, not only be made more appropriate in association with the decor, but also, if it was thought necessary, help her disappear as though her costume was a form of camouflage. A skilful wardrobe mistress indeed could almost make her invisible. On the other hand the Blue Widow could be used as a complimentary advertisement for a play. For the drama *"To the Ocean"*, for example, in association with the theatre's

[28] costume department, and building on her nickname and her accessory or attribute, the blue handkerchief, she wore a broad-skirted blue robe that was supported on a wire frame, accompanied by a purple hat in the shape of a whelk-shell that brought to mind a spiral staircase. Thus she aligned herself with a restless, sky-reflecting blueness, imaginary submarine-life and the towers that were being currently constructed to see the distant hypothetical blue sea.

Eventually, as could be expected, the theatre audience not only tolerated her, but enjoyed her presence, cheering and applauding her entrance, and becoming indeed upset and restless if she was absent.

If the Blue Widow of Denderon was the first recorded Steady-State Player, then her example was soon copied in other places, and just seven examples can be given here to demonstrate the range, the tenacity, the bizarre nature, the seriousness, and indeed the banality of the phenomenon.

A middle-aged man, a banker and a money-lender, who had travelled from Usaquay, a city of canals, took to sitting to one side of the stage at Fillering, and as the theatre audience became used to him, he grew emboldened to take off his clothes, garment by garment, over a period of several months until he was absolutely naked. Not having any more clothes to remove, he began to pose in more and more exotic, not to say anatomically revealing positions, until the management were obliged to ask him to leave, and he was banned from attending the theatre. After an absence of several weeks, and with some trickery, he returned to his old place, at the right of the stage, and proceeded to carve away at the skin on his chest to reveal the palpitating organs beneath a blood-stained rib-cage. After stripping and after revealing the intimate secrets of his body, his final recourse for attention was to denude himself of his flesh. Truly he was a consummate and determined player in the stakes of self-revelation. He was carried screaming from the theatre. Whether his heart-rending cries were because of his forced removal from the arena of his self-display, or because of the intense pain he must have been suffering, are truly debatable. It was later officially stated that he had died of a gangrenous infection. The theatre elephants, those intense devotees of Performance Drama, argued that the banker died of heartache brought on by forced abstinence from Gestures Drama participation. They declared that he had given Gestures Drama a pound of flesh. The man had truly tried to reveal his heart.

The theatre at Quitony had a Steady-State performer who fanned herself so regularly and rhythmically at deep stage left, that audiences believed her to be a clever automaton.

The Gertround Theatre humoured a large fat man who lay on a low couch with his feet illuminated by a candle floating in a dish of water. To signal the end of a performance, the stage performers ceremonially surrounded him and blew out the candle. With his feet unilluminated, the man could feel free to walk away in darkness.

The Yellow Theatre at Jickery humoured a woman who ate a light meal throughout a performance. Her six course supper was brought in by costumed waiters from a local eating-house and was timed to synchronise with the six-part drama on stage. After a while the drama was adapted to suit the meal, ending with the miming of a red hot poker being thrust down the throat of a major player and a red hot poker being thrust into a glass of the woman's brandy.

The Popliar Gestures Theatre suffered a Steady-State performer who stroked a patient animal on his lap. The lap-beast could have been a cat, save it occasionally squawked like a parrot, and had to have its diaper changed every 49 minutes.

The trick among Steady-State Performers was to do as much as possible to get noticed, but as little as possible to disturb the performance. Steady-State Performers who totally distracted an audience's attention could not be tolerated, though it is true that in some locations, they became so popular as mascots or talismans that theatre managements could not do without them, and to control the phenomenon, they fabricated these parasites from their own casts. The theatre manager Zackerlay referred to them as *"dirty lampreys*

[30] *attached to rainbow trout"*, and it may be true that at his theatre at
Bristowe, he knifed such a parasitising irritant, a young man who
dressed himself as a mermaid in the theatre latrines. To control and
forestall self-indulgent replacements, Zackerlay dressed a theatre
extra as a cook in a playhouse he leased at Whitelies that was
performing a drama of cannibalism. And he employed two acting
students as menagerie-keepers at Festinghead in a performance
that considered the world to be a zoo. And he paid a pittance to a
draughtsman at Vikty to sit on the stage and draw the participants
in acts of self-conscious conspiracy.

Three hooded men played a very quiet and carefully rehearsed game
of controlivo on the edge of the stage at Ghosting, and at Fresterling,
a corpse was put on the stage at the start of a performance and
removed at the end, with such repeated regularity, that until indeed
the corpse was situated with all due ceremony, the play could not
start, and until it was removed, it could not finish. It was kept a secret
whether the corpse was real or fake, or indeed a cast member. Various
devices were tried by the audience to discern the truth, including the
ignition of gunpowder. A definitive opinion was never forthcoming.

At Groompere a Steady-State player was permanently employed to
sit and look at a candle-lit effigy of Rowley.

At Lugga where the performance on a summer evening did not
begin until midnight, the management kept a Steady-State player
in attendance to sit or stand throughout the day on the completely
empty and unused stage to indicate that the theatre would be open
for business in the evening.

Theatres in the Southern Territories that did not continuously employ
a Steady-State player were considered closed for the season, whilst a
manager who shunned such traditions at Grior was considered
bankrupt and his theatre had to be abandoned. Offering free seats for
performances did not help. The manager's refusal to acknowledge
theatrical tradition was considered unacceptable, even inimical, to the
community in general.

47. A curious prophetic move to maybe introduce sound into Gestures Drama
entertainments occurred at Redowning, when three young players made
especial use of the opening and closing of the mouth.
In this performance, whenever a character made a motion which
intimated a movement to vocalise, the second character would clamp
his hand over the mouth of the first, and the third player would
demonstrably block his ears, all three working together in quick
unison in a routine that was both adroit and amusing. The three
players would then look at the audience from over their shoulders, as
much as to say, *"Did you experience anything illegal?"*, and blink their
apparent innocence like monkeys before a bright light.

48. An obscene gesture to indicate slow self-stimulation without enjoyment
and the likelihood of a sterile ejaculate, was introduced at Stealing Common.
This gesture was regarded as a criticism of the present governing
body of the Centre Edge who had lost all confidence in itself.

49. Three young mathematicians excited by symbolic numerology, wrote a
paper on Gestures Drama arithmetic.
It was generally now perceived that a significant counting system
associated with the number seven and its multiples had been
established by persistent usage. Performance lengths, stage
proportions, prop-numbers, Gestures Drama vocabulary and
structures of choreography were all seven-based. The
comprehension that this was so was deemed to have a unifying value
for a Gestures Theatre seeking rigour, discipline and approval. It
began to be voiced that the mythical Rowley had been seven feet tall.

50. Forever associated with a desire for "the Moderate Way", the urban
communities of the Centre Edge wished to curb what they saw to be the
excesses of Gestures Theatre.
Its freely developing growth, largely unregulated from within, and
certainly not regulated from without, irritated their sensibilities.
They attempted first of all to make a move to regulate the Gestures

[32] Drama companies through the only perceivable representative body, the Jatchett Registry, which, to avoid plagiarism in the industry and to look after authors' and actors' rights, had instituted a loose book-keeping system. But the Jatchett Registry was a voluntary institution arranged for mutual benefit and had no legal standing or constitution that could be enforced. The supporters of *The Moderate Way*, lead by the ledger-clerk Antimious Bricker, surreptitiously researched the Jatchett Registry's very incomplete archives to find a means to legislate. Not finding the tools for the restrictions they wanted, they started to interfere with various public and private sources of income and support for Gestures Drama by forms of persuasion which some might call intimidation. They contrived to limit certain public services to Gestures Drama managers and supporters.

Antimious Bricker drew up a list of limitations that included a refusal to collect street horse-dung, to limit the cropping and felling of dangerous trees, to delay the implementation of the maintenance of roads and tracks, to introduce adverse re-routing of open drains, and to enforce a biased selected use of public lighting to make access to the homes and workplaces of Gestures Drama supporters difficult, problematic and possibly dangerous, and certainly aesthetically unsatisfactory.

In some cases, to rid themselves of these restrictions and prohibitions, theatre managers succumbed to the pressure, and agreed to pay small fees that both parties agreed to consider as theatre taxes.

Emboldened by their modest successes, supporters of *The Moderate Way*, often now known as the Moderators, considered controlling Gestures Drama by insisting on the issue of architectural licenses to build theatres, and by pursuing bylaws rarely evoked. Again Bricker drew up a list, which included taxes on balconies, windows overlooking public streets, stages over three feet high, red cloth, fish-meals, seats numbering a collection in excess of two hundred, and an entrance penalty fee on arches under ten feet high. Bricker's daughter, Mitchette, even considered issuing permits to use the name Rowley.

To soften the force of their interference as a personal vendetta, the Brickers, father and daughter, institutionalised their activities, becoming the official main sponsors of AGDL - the Anti-Gestures Drama Legislation. It was suggested at first that the institutionalised impediments should be considered to be payments made on a voluntary basis proportional to a theatre's income, to be paid at every company's individual discretion, to be collected to service theatrical education, in regard to a public sense of charity. This of course served to create animosities between theatres, since, if paid at all, everyone tried to minimise their contribution, or paid in such a way as to be entirely out of proportion to their box-office successes. This inter-theatre animosity was something the Moderators were pleased to exploit. And when, because any interfering alternative was worse, by force of habit, voluntary subscriptions became more or less acceptable, the Moderators made them compulsory.

Having gained such a foothold, the Moderators began to agitate for control of the Gestures Drama theatrical material, wishing to read scenarios, asking to regularise vocabulary in the public good for decent speech amongst young people, limit words of more than four syllables to avoid pomposity, and censor foreign words to keep local language unadulterated.

They eventually had the audacity to ask for a seat at all casting-sessions to observe and, if they found it necessary, which Mitchette Bricker frequently did, to have a casting vote to regulate labour. Mitchette Bricker became such a frequent figure sitting on the edge of the stage with her black note-books, that she was nicknamed Rowley's widow and mercilessly lampooned. She was indeed considered for a time, with her lips blackened from the graphite of her continually sucked pencils, as a Steady-State Player.

[34]   *51. In the Southern Long Country around Cassawart, a group of energetic*
cultural ambassadors initiated a funding situation that encouraged the
formation of large Gestures Drama Companies.

They proposed a system that in return for seven new "public"
productions a year and a minimum of 98 performances every 365 days,
they would supply funds to design, construct and maintain Gestures
Drama performance spaces that could employ a minimum of 14 front
stage performers and 28 backstage supporting staff. The companies
were free to exploit their stages, performers and staff on the making of
their own "private" productions in the remaining days of the year.

Fifteen companies applied for funding, twelve received the necessary
economic help to commence production, and after eighteen months,
with three companies not being able to satisfy the requirements, nine
companies were thriving and successful.

A year later, newly appointed cultural ambassadors that included the
two Witten Brothers, Erzo and Hattan, further tightened the regulations. The companies dropped to seven which was considered appropriate and sustainable, and a two-way respect and dedication was
established between companies and ambassadors which strongly
affected the company managements and the material they produced.
The rigour for discipline and practice was strong, with the performers
voluntarily denying themselves speech or any vocalisations on and off
stage if their Gesture vocabulary could suffice to communicate their
meaning. In three companies this characteristic became exceptional and
the performers took vows of complete silence on and off stage whilst
performing what were to be called the Ambassador's Performances.

One management company called itself the Rowley Representatives,
though detractors nicknamed them *The Ambassadors' Dogs*. They
asked of their employees a complete vow of silence for five years for
all the front and back stage staff, making exceptions only for
bereavements, marriages and births. Communication was
infrequently permitted through the written word if that which needed
to be communicated was either abstract, or of such a complexity as to
deny comprehension in any other way, though all such written

communications had to be made on officially recognised blue-lined [35] yellow paper called *"the yellow sheets"*. At first much *"yellow-sheet"* communication was accumulated, but continual practice slowly minimised the load. It was insisted that all *"yellow-sheet"* material should be collected and was deemed to be the property of the company.

The Rowley Representatives Company assumed a special dress, a hooded yellow robe, marked with loose red threads sewn into the cloth. They shaved their bodies, walked barefoot, and abstained from sexual intercourse unless it was expressly undertaken to produce children, an activity itself made into a publicly witnessed ritualised performance. The *"twenty-one gestures to accompany sexual intercourse to produce a child"* became both an elegant theatrical classic to be learnt and used by shy lovers, and a ribald farce, exploited for amusement by the sensual and the exhibitionist.

Some performers of the Rowley Representatives claimed, as a result of the very strict and regulated and disciplined regime, to be able to defy gravity. Whether by supernatural means or by trickery, they convinced their audiences that their claims could be substantiated. The asceticism, and the sense of a closed dedicated community, attracted many acolytes, and after two years, the performances of the Rowley Representatives were eagerly anticipated and intensively debated. The auditoria, always full, developed a system of allocating tickets that was organised on grounds other than money and patronage, but relative to patience, age, merit and enthusiasm.

It is a sad curiosity that such a well-behaved and self-disciplined dedicated company should have attracted the displeasure of The Moderators of the Urban Centre Edge. The extreme activities of self-denial of the Rowley Representatives Company made the Moderators feel uncomfortable. They felt obliged to interfere. The Brickers, father and daughter, accused the Company of immodesty suitable for prosecution. Pressure was brought to bear on the funding ambassadors in the form of personal threats. Propaganda was released to excite antagonistic opinion. Angry and resentful that such a success story in

[36] asceticism, moral tone, general example and aesthetic excellence should be subject to the prejudices of this restricting body, the ambassadors, lead by the Witten Brothers, dramatically and abruptly withdrew their funding. They thought it preferable to finish the exercise on a high position of honour and respect than be debilitated in slow stages by making impossible compromises. The Rowley Representatives' Company were immediately forced to close the theatres and dismiss their staff. The Moderators were shocked, and declared the ambassadors' actions to be immodest, and demanded negotiations to be reopened, but these were adamantly refused.

The rivalry between the Brickers, father and daughter, and the two Witten brothers, escalated, and became personal. An equally shocked public whose loyalty was exemplary, rioted, dragged Moderators from their homes and lynched two elderly male extremists. They kidnapped Mitchette Bricker and burnt off her long hair, saying it was an item of excess and an offence to moderation. In retaliation, the Moderators formed armed bands to protect their lives and property, dressing their members in blue uniforms stolen from a theatre company's dressing rooms. This was the start of the police force later to be called The Gestures Drama Blue Police. Antimious Bricker became their marshal. He shaved his head in sympathetic solidarity with his daughter. He was considered to be an intemperate man.

52. The first plans to build a stage to be called The Yellow Flag with respect to Rowley's initial legendary, but probably apocryphal gesture, were instituted at Precedenter.

This theatre specialised in performances at night by very brightly lighting performers against black velvet or indeed against the moonless night itself, developing a characteristic which later became to be known as *Black Box Theatre*.

53. A company of gesture actors in Benarther, perhaps characterised by their benefactor, Korfer, who was confined to lying very still in bed after a paralysing fall from a nutmeg tree, developed several scenarios of what can only be described as Minimalist Activity.

They gestured with the eyes and the fingers and, for those patient enough to watch assiduously, with very very slow movements of the torso and the hips.

These body movements were accomplished, it was said, searching for an appropriate metaphor, at the same speed that the sun-shadow of a nutmeg tree moved over the face of the earth. For this reason and with acknowledgement to the incapacity of their benefactor, they were later known as The Nutmeg Company. Their activity was prized for its extreme dramatic economy. It attracted admirers and eventually spawned imitators, one group of which, practising on a wooden-plank stage in a darkened cave at Jablock, to all intents and purposes, and certainly as perceived by the uninitiated, remained entirely still, dressed in extravagant costumes. The costumes often made of paper and feathers, could afford to be extremely delicate, detailed and fragile because of the minimal movement of the wearers. Part of the critical appraisal for such a performance was to discuss what movement in fact had taken place, because it was indeed certain that the seven participants in a seven hour performance were certainly not in the same places on stage at the end of the performance as they had been at the start.

54. A gesture that a torturer might use to inspire trust that he will not knowingly inflict pain.
The word *"torturer"* in Gorindeer was pronounced the same way as the name of a distrusted local politician currently in office. This silent play on unspoken words was seen as a veiled attempt by inference, to introduce vocalisation into Gestures Theatre.

In this drama, whilst the rest of the performer's body writhed and shook with menace, the very sharp razor he held high in the air, was gripped with exacting stillness in the light created by a mirror that reflected the sun. The mirror was held by the performer's naked assistant, a boy, whose body, from the nipples to the knees, was splashed in imitation blood. The prologue and epilogue of the piece were called *The Blood Verifications*. The boy squatted on stage

[38] before the start of the performance with a pestle and a mortar and manufactured the false blood from beetroot and red currants. He then wrapped a white cloth around his head and shoulders and another around his lower legs, and he splashed himself with the red juice. He hung the spuriously blood-stained white clothes on a ceremonial rail in the centre of the stage and awaited the arrival of his master. After the performance the boy permitted his body to be licked by women and children from the audience. It was a gesture to allay fears of real violence, and to demonstrate artifice.

55. As a memorial work to celebrate the Witten Brothers and the beneficent support of the Cultural Ambassadors of Cassawart, three plays were performed in a winter season, whose substance was distilled from the collected written communications of the "yellow-sheets" of the Rowley Representatives Players.
It was an opportunity to examine what was considered to be incommunicable by gesture alone, and an insight into the private life of gestures players. Permission to communicate in writing on the "yellow-sheets" was only allowed in cases of the death of a child, a marriage across a vocal language barrier and a complicated birth. The Witten Brothers, Erzo and Hattan, wearing theatrical costume, were invited to be present in the audience. They sat on a raised dais, rather like Steady-State players. Erzo, the younger brother, was excited enough by the honour to consider an ambition to become a true participant of a Gestures Drama performance. He grew his hair long and started to wear furs, sometimes presenting a ludicrous figure in hot weather, sweating and red-faced in his finery.

56. A set of cooking gestures comprehensible to all, was performed on a small stage in a theatre in the Wolden.
This performance became very popular perhaps because it was regarded as a welcome relief to theatre watchers concerned at having to visit a Gestures performance in the knowledge that its intentions were supposed to be subversive or instructive or aesthetic. The event

had humour. In gesture, the metaphorical cook burnt his fingers, ate [39] spun sugar off a spoon, swallowed a live eel and kissed his mother-in-law after eating wild garlic. The gestures used to indicate the concept of the mother-in-law were often imitated, parodied and reverently quoted. A disparaged mother-in-law for a time was called an Opsilion after the lead performer.

57. The first totally acknowledged classic Gestures Drama Playhouse was built in Botolphy according to the currently perceived rules and rituals of the genre.
It had a free-standing stage erected under the effigy of a barking dog, and was surrounded by 343 seats, forty-nine of them arranged on the southern side which was considered to be the side of day-time privilege best lit by the sun. All stage properties used in the production, to be numbered in any multiple of seven, were to be displayed on stage before the performance. All performers washed and dressed on stage to make a watchable prologue, and they were clapped and kissed afterwards, if deemed worthy, in a procedure known as *The Appreciation*. At the premiere performance of a work called *The Rowley Dog*, every audience member, on being seated, was given an elephant mask made of grey crepe paper, and a terrier puppy. Some two hundred dogs were returned at the end of the performance. Five of them were dead, suffocated by excessive attention.

58. A branch of Gestures Theatre became a platform for what could only be described as educational drama.
Citizens from the North whose pragmatism was infamous, reacted strongly against what they perceived to be pure and unnecessary aestheticism. They wanted Gestures Drama activity to have a defined and recognisably practical purpose. Maybe this demand was made out of a need to be able to communicate what they had experienced directly, and without abstract vocabulary in which they were not practised and with which, if they were honest, they felt uncomfortable, if not embarrassed, to use. They eventually repudiated foreign companies and formed their own.

[40] Amongst the early examples of what they had to offer were Gestures Dramas devoted to childcare and infant welfare. These performances had a proselytising attitude to encourage breast feeding and natural birth processes related to a dissatisfaction with the region's low local birth-rates. Their gestures vocabulary was full of slow and peaceful copulatory activity, ritualised labour pains, breast-feeding, and child rearing. No child was permitted by local statute to appear on stage, so a range of young female actors playing babies and young children developed with extraordinary skills in performing such concepts as Bitoff's *"the awakened embryo"*, Poringhay's *"the first responses of intelligence"*, and Levenscape's *"the primary walking-steps"*. It is true that infant mortality decreased in many cities of the North around this time, but there are many more benevolent factors to be acknowledged to account for this phenomenon other than Gestures Drama.

The activity, though locally successful, did not travel so well, the opinions of communities further South being that the dramas were too predictable and too didactic, though the gesturing skills were respected. It was suggested that these performances were mimetic, and what sort of true and worthy appreciation was possible if the applause could only be limited to praising what was a trueness to life, and not created from the imagination, for the former could never equal its idol, and the latter had to be surely a product of the most valuable thing in existence, which was indeed the human imagination.

Five or six of the young female actors travelled with their talents, expanding their vocabulary, but the results were of dubious value. Three settled in Utticanet and formed a company whose acted innocence was attractive, but, by degrees, in response to audience demand, they became corrupted, introducing vulgarity and strained sexuality, such that commentators described their activity as pedophiliac, an accusation not repudiated when two of the performers became very wealthy, gratifying private patrons in acts of simulated child pornography.

Perhaps associated with the move towards a greater didactic theatre [41] of gestures, were the companies around the Jaddermore Basin next to the Jadder Morrains who began to specialise in the gestures of animals. A Company at Wretcherly gained an enviable reputation for bird gesturing and mimicry, most particularly for a programme of four events that were imitations of *"a chained Blue Cockatoo preening its tail"*, *"a Fresh-water Batteak Heron eating a Sea-water Eel"*, *"a Crimson Crested Flamingo swallowing a female Crayfish with eggs"*, and *"a Sunrise Humming-bird drinking honey-water from a Tallirand Flower"*. Based on an admiration for the sheer detailed observational virtuosity of the performances, various members of the company were invited to travel, but they curiously misunderstood the nature of their success and began to introduce real life animals on stage, training them to gesture like humans. A group of athletic young men specialising in the complex gesturing of primates, introduced young monkeys into their act, and immediately the phenomenon went curiously sour, for the suspension of disbelief possible in the absence of real animals, entirely collapsed when the reality was directly compared to the artifice.

59. In a performance at Trentan'all, an event occurred that proved to be of great significance for the whole future of Gestures Drama. An actor, gesturing astonishment, fell down a trap-well by accident.

This actor disappeared from view, and he howled in pain for a full minute before being rescued and comforted. He had broken a bone in his foot. The audience was shocked. The company was renowned for its efficient acrobatics. Was this in fact a deliberate gestural artifice or was it indeed an accident? The shocked silence in an audience that was used to converse during performances was a surprise novelty. The company exploited the event and all its reactions in subsequent performances. If the first event was indeed a mistake then subsequent vocalising at the performance of the fall at the trap-well were indeed practised and fake.

[42] The repeated howl of pain at Trenta is regarded as the first recorded deliberate vocalisation in Gestures Drama. What is curious and important is the fact that the vocalisation, though primitive and onomatopoeic, happened out of sight. To have had a Gestures Performer vocalise at all is revolutionary, to have had that vocalisation appear visible, gesture and sound together would have closed the theatre and invited prosecution, though quite how the legal accusation could have been worded and applied is not easy to say.

For a time the vocalisation activity was too revolutionary to be imitated, though the theatre at Trenta exploited its novelty value, and extended its run of the relevant drama to eighteen weeks. The performances drew large crowds who hardly paid any attention to the gestures activity that led to the now simulated fall and cry, but simply waited with baited breath for the fall to happen. The rest of the Gestures Drama at Trenta almost became irrelevant, for the audience had seen what they had come to see, and the crescendo of conversation and chatter after *"the fall and cry"* completely spoiled concentration for actors and audience alike. Not that many people were worried. Towards the end of the eighteen week run in fact the drama was shortened and in the last four days finished absolutely at the trap-door fall, making the simulated cry of pain the finale of the piece.

The significance of the event lent itself eventually to subsequent Gestures Drama vocabulary. Dramas with vocalisation, which at first were very few, because they were so daring, and seriously broke theatrical convention, were called *"Fall and Cry Dramas"*, and any significant activity in any Gestures Drama that disturbed an audience were referred to as an *"After the Fall"* phenomenon.

There was official talk of penalising the actor who had started such a revolution, of fining his company, and of closing the theatre where he performed. None of which happened, because it was considered at this time that vocalisation in Gestures Drama was an aberrant event, unlikely to be repeated. The actor who had created all this furore, Bendeckie Albignal, had received a excessive amount of attention, even adulation, certainly notoriety. He was to resurface in the history of Gestures Drama, seeking more of the same. In the meantime he persuaded audiences to remember his great achievement by limping, both on and off stage. Constructing a trap-door set on a corn-cart, which already had a drop-shoot for thrashed grain, he toured a dramatised version of his stage accident. He accumulated enough finances after a year to build himself a small stage at Arkeeness, one of the cities along the Great Bend Country, where he enlarged his company to five persons, and became even more wealthy, though his activities were seen as something apart from any development of Gestures Theatre. It would indeed be some five years before this sort of event, in any guise of orthodoxy, would be repeated, and a considerable time into the future before an even greater break in tradition would be enacted when the first heard-and-seen synchronisation vocalisation would occur.

60. Ten white-clad, elderly men edged themselves onto an empty darkened stage from the right-hand side, the side that was always supposed to entertain the entry of the villain.

Shuffling their feet, but in organised unison, they entered in a wide curve, all in a synchronous movement, nodding their heads together like absent-minded, imprisoned invalids, with their hands forever lifting up at regular intervals to cup their eyes along the level of the eyebrows.

This performance was to be regarded as a unified gesture of despair in a play designed to give mixed signals about the responsibility of the state. The composite gesture could conceivably be a movement to indicate a look into the far distance, which metaphorically could also be considered to be a look into the future. Detractors of a pragmatic turn of mind might say the gesture was only a motion to shade the eyes from the great glare of the sun or a bright light of unfamiliar origin. Maybe despair could be sometimes considered to be analogous to the glare of a bright light of unfamiliar origin.

[44] *61. In a small theatre on the edge of The Wattle a very accomplished actor used minimal gestures to conjure sheer elegance without committal to any dogma, credo, belief, message or philosophy.*

The performance was advertised as The Table Drama. The actor sat at a table and peeled, quartered and ate an apple, drank a glass of water, then read a short text on political suffrage and then lit a candle. In the course of this activity, he brushed away an imaginary fly from his face seven times. He frequently glanced into the auditorium to bring the audience into his confidence, and demonstrate that he was always aware of their attention.

The significance of the actor's activity passed over the heads of most members of the audience who expected to be entertained with narrative and action, and not atmosphere, ambience or feeling. Some of the audience members, prepared to be patient, looked for especial meaning in the chair and the table, the apple and the apple knife, the book and the candle. They deliberated on the topics of domesticity, sustenance, the origins of life, violence, instruction and enlightenment. But there was a scattering of cognoscenti who realised that they were watching consummate perfection of gesture. Some of these audience members left the theatre weeping, others tried to hire the actor to appear in front of more sophisticated audiences.

On the seventh night of the intended run of twenty-one performances, six elderly women found the actor changing his shoes after the performance in a rehearsal room, and unabashed, kissed and embraced him warmly, even sensually. A little later, an elderly man associated with the women, approached the actor in the empty, deserted, damp field opposite the theatre where the actor had gone to urinate, and stabbed him in the belly. The murder weapon was the apple knife that had appeared on stage. At last, fulfilling prophesies, a truly significant and relevant event had been invented for *"The Innocent Space"* opposite a Gestures Theatre. The actor, without uttering a word or a cry, bled to death on the damp grass.

This is the first authenticated record of the violent death of an actor associated with Gestures Drama relevant to his profession. His name, already renowned, and a password for excellence and devotion to craft, became a superstitious evocation of death. No-one, certainly no-one in the gestures theatre profession, was now prepared to mention him by his given name. He was always henceforth to be referred to as *"The Table-Player"*, and well-researched studies of his work were related to the many mythical events and incidents of history associated with diners at a table, with last meals and with significant last suppers, all of which implied sacrifice that usually included an element of betrayal and certainly a cruel loss of life.

The elderly assassin, Mensa Strobbor, who had committed his murder in *"The Innocent Space"*, did not resist arrest. He never went to trial, but quietly accepted a life-long imprisonment that he appeared to turn into an entirely voluntary act. He was determined to behave, in the forced circumstances of his small cell, like his hero in the activity of his last performance. He contrived to find the artefacts of the performance he had witnessed, a chair, a table, an apple, a glass of water, a book and a candlestick, and spent his long lonely days, acting. He was not permitted a naked flame for his candle, or a knife for his apple, so he perfected his activities in order to do without such props, and thus manoeuvred himself into a superior position to his idol, for his world of make-believe was that much more imaginary. His example possibly became more celebrated than the example set by the man who he had murdered. It was an act to reduce reality in Gestures Drama to a minimum, if not to completely eradicate it.

For seven years, Mensa Strobbor proved to be such a model prisoner that the authorities, who never ceased to watch him with admiration, trusted him enough to permit him a naked flame and a knife, but he rejected them. He also asked that the other properties be removed from his cell. Perhaps his greatest achievement lay in

[46] his ability to arrange his body in a sitting position without a chair with perfect composure before his now invisible table for hours at a time. He now made a request that he should not be watched since his perfected performance did not need an audience. He had himself blind-folded. After the seven year preparation, it was no longer necessary for the performance to be watched by anyone, even by himself. He request not to be watched, was refused for security reasons, but his immediate jailers restricted their observations to a minimum, briefly looking through the peep-hole in his cell-door only once a day. It was not enough, Strobbor blinded himself to lessen the possibility of witnessing his activity. He pulled his eyes out of their sockets with his fingers.

Seven months later, the prisoner, sitting at his imaginary table on his imaginary chair, quietly died. He was 98, at 14 times 7 this was a most appropriate age for a Gestures Drama performer. He passed away so unobtrusively that his imaginatively seated body remained undisturbed for seven hours. His death was only discovered when his jailer saw a fly sitting on his cheek that did not get brushed away.

62. An actor would not be told that to make the gesture of pretending to write when writing, was not good enough. In the presently developing characteristics of Gestures Drama theatre, he could never accept that to do, rather than to gesture to do, was what was required of him.

In pique the actor burnt down the theatre where he performed. It was the first theatrical burning of a Gestures Drama Building. It was to become a tradition, and a tradition to relate to the resistance to Gestures Theatre becoming real.

63. Areas of exploitation for Gestures Drama began to proliferate and the mythologising of public events in living memory became popular.

These public events could be staid re-enactments like the reconstruction of the wedding of Gloriander and Hilt, or the funeral procession of Potlocki, but most of them were re-enactments of serious crimes, and became so numerous that it might be said they could constitute a genre in their own right called *Criminals Gesture Theatre*. Four examples could be considered representative: *The Chicken-Heads*, *The Gravity Children*, *The Baker's Daughter* and *Milk Whoring*, a melodrama, a tragedy, a comedy and a farce.

The play *The Chicken-Heads* was renowned for its animal-human metamorphosis and the density of its research conducted at judicial beheadings. It was based on a crime of twenty years before when a poultry farmer had become demented with ergotism contracted from inexpertly fermented rye-grass beer. He decapitated his eleven children, to replace their heads with the heads of chickens, to make them, he said, more productive at laying. The gestures on the stage that represented the change from human to chicken in the performers, all under twelve years of age, was alarming and deeply moving. The loss of conscionable reasoning to the greedy, jerking automatic responses of henhouse pecking orders, and the repetitive movements of unthinking instinctive behaviour, was appalling in its implications.

The second play, *The Gravity Children*, was renowned for its gestures of falling, rehearsed it was said from life, though it is still a puzzle how the actors managed to convey so apparently accurately a second by second appearance of the effects of falling. The performance was based on the activities of a child murderer whose advocate's defence was formed on the opinion that his client had been teaching his victims to fly.

The Baker's Daughter was a comedy involving fourteen separated parts of the human anatomy baked in pies. It was associated with a criminal incident in the Trethcorimond, when a pastry-maker inadvertently locked his unmarriagable daughter in an oven, and was accused of ridding himself of an unsaleable asset.

The farce *Milk Whoring* was developed from the trial of a schoolmaster who ran a wet-nurse business for octogenarian scholars who had lost their teeth and could not chew but only suck for sustenance.

These plays were sometimes criticised for being no more than a repository of stock gestures theatre clichés, many of which had

[48] accumulated around the movements associated with frantic sexual courtship, grief, regret and consolation, activities themselves associated with the plagues that repeatedly devastated the valleys of the Western Plain along all the navigable rivers. It may be that these gestures associated with deep pain and extreme violence were cathartic, artificial re-enactments of painful events to keep the real painful events at bay. Audiences became very familiar with this vocabulary, and would expect and anticipate the gestures, demanding a familiar recognisable gesture every three or four minutes. In the auditorium they collectively copied each gesture from the stage with heroic over-statement. A cuff to the ear for a simple admonishment, a finger to the brow to indicate the arrival of an idea, a slicing blow to the throat to suggest a death, squatting to relieve both the bowel and an evil thought, hands held behind the ears to suggest loss, not simply of hearing, but of understanding, folded arms to suggest determination, thigh-slapping to indicate laughter, genital-cupping to suggest sexual abstinence, plugging the anus with a thumb to indicate loose bowels and uncontrollable excess, bending double to indicate cramp, the onset of disease or pregnancy and the pains of ignorance, leaning to the left from the hips to indicate humiliated masculinity, leaning to the right to suggest femininity triumphant. Ballahurst counted some four hundred of these gestures, and concocted a performance at Yallope called *"In Praise of Signs"*, where all four hundred gestures were used with only a slapping of the back of the head in between each gesture to suggest the preposition "and".

The success of these plays resided in the audience's familiarity with the narrative, drama, location and gesture. It is interesting that these four dramas, quite truly representative, had so many features in common; the female as victim, the iconography of animals, a prevalence for disasters occurring to children, and a propensity to set dramas in rural environments. This last characteristic itself, for a time in the West, developed what could be described as a Romantic Rustic Gestures Theatre, with a vocabulary of the so-called romance of the simple life,

with characters pretending to be milkmaids, pigmen, shepherds, **[49]**
farmer's wives and cowherds. It is however to be noticed that the cost
of the milkmaid's on-stage dress at Tregorran was deliberately
advertised as exorbitant, and the equivalent of what a milkmaid living
in Jaimonde or Illnature might earn in three lifetimes.

*64. An actor from Stock created such powerful weather effects on stage, that
with the slightest gesture, like turning up his coat collar or holding a spittle-
wetted finger in the air, or taking off his shirt, he could persuade an audience
to feel the blast of an icy wind, a summer breeze before rain, or the rich blaze
of an autumn afternoon sun.*
Summoning the idea of a cold rainstorm in a Gestures Drama about
The Winter Queen, this very accomplished actor sent an audience home
with wracking coughs. It is said that a quarter of this audience died
within the next few days of pneumonia and bronchitis. But this may
be a pardonable exaggeration made in praise of a formidable talent.

*65. A gesture to demonstrate the height of an imagined tower to be built on the
edge of a lake, such that its reflection would suggest the tower was twice as
high as its builders could claim it to be.*
The performance was politically motivated, so most of the audience
were not prepared to suspend disbelief and sympathise with what the
young actor had to offer. Speculating algebraiscists, mathematicians and
trigonometricians enjoyed his performances. Three admirers attended
so regularly, they were regarded as Steady-State Players, and we invited
to sit on the stage holding set-squares as attributes of their trade.

*66. An orthodox gesture to indicate a bad smell is to conventionally pinch the
nose. But from such a gesture it is scarcely possible to gauge the flavour,
quality and strength of a smell. If the intention was to demonstrate that a
smell was issuing from a decaying human corpse, how come the audience
believed that the source of the smell was merely human flatulence? Surely this
must be tragedy descending to banal comedy. A company at Threadneedle,
investigated the problem and arrived at an abstract solution.*

[50] All smells at Threadneedle were to be represented by wooden pyramids about a foot high placed in the centre of the stage by a stagehand in a costume designed to represent the wind. A pink pyramid would represent the very best of smells, a yellow pyramid the most undesirable. In all, some thirty-four coloured pyramids were brought into play, hopefully making up a spectrum of all conceived scents and odours. The Gestures Performers would make their approaches to the pyramid, and with elaborate mimes and motions conjure a picture such that the audience's nostrils were filled with the relevant perfume. To add degrees of difficulty, the gesturer added complications, like deliberate degrees of lying, suggestions that the smells were cross-adulterated, that they had sexual identities, and that they were often colour-blind so could not recognise their order in the colour-coding of the pyramids.

67. In response to a public competition, Rowley's orthodox costume and appearance was established.
Rowley was to be associated with wide-hipped, white padded trousers, a pot belly, a blue jacket, reddened and greasy cheeks, thin lips, a long yellow nose, scanty hair, a modestly padded codpiece, black-gloved hands carrying a yellow flag, and white or yellow built-up wooden shoes. Sometimes he wore a narrow-brimmed, high crowned hat the same colour as his jacket.
Not to be outdone by such a concentration of Rowley as a man, female performers developed a persona for Rowley as a woman, save the pot belly frequently invoked pregnancy, and too often, the resulting figure had no dignity, and merely appeared as a man with fake breasts and a blonde wig.
Debate also developed as to the way in which Rowley was permitted to move on stage. Normally he was rooted to the spot, and his large wooden shoes emphasised this fact, but, of necessity, various dramas of his life and times insisted on his movement. Initially, persistently waving his flag with gestures starting from the elbow, he was carted

about the stage-space on a flatbed trolley pulled by two servants, who were sometimes dressed as twins. These twin servants, appearing so frequently, were permitted to have identities, and were named Astrier and Proluxer, and their performance was praised on the excellence of an absolute synchronisation they shared in every gesture, down to the blinking of their eye-lids. They often had control over the behaviour of the Gestures Drama dog, and, in this capacity, referring back to an early Gestures Drama event, could be known as *The Dog Twins Players*.

Eventually, hoping for greater freedom of movement, a Rowley-impersonator at Graverstone abandoned the flatbed trolley, relegating Astrier and Proluxer to develop routines on their own if they hoped to survive as stage-characters. The Graverstone Rowley Impersonator shuffled about in sideways movements on stage as though his feet were joined together, and only permitted himself freedom of movement from the hips upwards.

Another Rowley performer, this time at Mapperly, respected the tradition of the stiff Rowley icon but allowed his impersonation to move like a figure on a gameboard, to the front and to the side with one step at a time. No diagonal movements were permitted, and the body was always kept frontal to the audience. If the audience was seated on more than one side of the stage, then the theatre was orienteered towards the South, whence, it was said, Rowley originated, though the town of Rowley, being six hundred miles north of the Cumber Northern Perimeter, was obviously not to considered a Southern town. Perhaps the desire to make Rowley a Southerner, was relevant to the traditionally received notion that all innovations came from the South, especially innovations of an equivocal or dubious nature.

Rowley impersonations became common, and at least a dozen Gestures performance artists made themselves celebrated as a result. They extended their personifications off-stage, earning infamy, notoriety and fortunes in association with public events,

[52] public ceremonies and political careers. In three publicised cases, actors personifying Rowley respectively developed a pornographic franchise, a patriotic party claiming unacceptable ideas of genetic superiority, and the sponsorship of a new alcoholic drink made from yeasted feathers, familiarly to be called *"Rowley's Pleasure"*.

68. Nearly five years after the infamous "Fall and Cry" event at Trentan'all, two Gestures Theatre houses in the Great Bend country, with due warning to their audiences, advertised and performed an event called The Simple Onomatopoeia Show.

Both houses presented seven vocalisations promoted in a drama called *The Seven Calls of the Downright Man and his Dog*. The seven onomatopoeic sounds were advertised as two sounds of surprise, two screams, a sigh of relief, an intake of breath, and a whistle. The manager of one of the theatres was Bendeckie Albignal, the original gestures drama performer who had fallen down the trapdoor at the Trenta Theatre, and who had continued to try, with some considerable success, to subsequently limp himself into public notice. The other theatre house was managed by his nephew. The seven vocal parts of the performance were elaborately situated in complex gestural procedures, as though to embrace and perhaps smother the vocalisation, even convince an audience that they had not really heard anything at all. It was a clever ploy of subtle insinuation of the revolutionary novelties, and after a slow start, it reaped great rewards, because within a year it was certainly agreed that these two Albignal theatre houses could be said to have thoroughly planted the idea of legitimised sound into Gestures Theatre.

If the first important date of Vocalised Gestures Theatre began officially with the trapdoor event at Trenta, the second important date could be said to be the Saturday evening of the 1st July in the year of the Great Harnsett Marriage. On that evening the mayors and the marshals of the Quigley graced the Potadoorman theatre of Abignal's nephew. They brought their families and their parliaments. Such a public show of domestic and community support swayed all the local doubters, hesitaters, jeremiads, critics and cynics. Onomatopoeic vocalisation won a seal of approval.

Though in a way legitimised, it has to be said that initially, as though deliberately to travel slowly, onomatopoeia was used sparingly. It was initially reserved for set piece dramatic events or else put in what could be described as quotation marks. Nonetheless, performers and audience curiously waited for these moments, often advertised on stage in advance, with baited breath. There are many anecdotes surrounding this phenomenon, of which the swooning and fainting of audience members in anticipation of the vocalisations, was of minor notice. A company at Oakacaper was prone to stretch out the times of anticipation until elderly audience members suffered heart attacks and young members started throwing eggs, though nobody brought eggs to a theatre unless they hoped to throw them. There were fires at Mockling and Starch which were said to have been caused by the overdue anticipation of vocalisation, and at Woppiter, audience members pleaded with the theatre management to shorten the anticipation time by offering bribes, including sexual favours; a middle-aged woman lifted her skirts and jumped astride the manager's neck. A stage author was throttled at Trusset, and a theatre manager stabbed at Lourmatta for tampering with what came to be known as *"the anticipation programme"*.

When the vocalisations arrived within a Gestures Drama, they were exuberantly applauded, and this applause became an awaited feature in itself, the performers leaving a space for it, expecting it and developing a gestures routine when it was happening. At Skeptisson, in a performance of a work called The Howler, in appreciation of the multiple baying of what could have sounded like a wounded dog, though nobody seemed to care to want to know the sound's origin, the applause lasted half an hour. The onomatopoeia with its attendant applause came to be known as *The Clapping Act* and was often considered to be the highlight of a performance. Six months

[54] after the famous evening at Potadoorman, Fender Pendlebury and Clovis Adamantine put on a performance at Cloosebery, simply called *The Clapping Act* which was just that, forty-nine minutes of tumultuous clapping with some screaming and banging and shouting to occasionally vary the noise characteristic. The license to make organised appreciative noise en masse in public, appeared for a time to be like the effect of suddenly removing a drug from the prohibited list, or like a public gag unexpectedly removed, but curiously in retrospective no one had felt that before the liberating event they had missed the drug or had indeed been gagged.

In the first onomatopoeic Gestures Theatre performances, the performers were obliged to go into hiding on the stage to conduct their vocalisations.

Because of the precedent of the first Gesture Drama vocalisation happening down a stage trapdoor at Trenta, audiences needed to see the players, prior to vocalisation, go demonstrably into concealment, initially into a pit or space beneath the stage. Later, it became acceptable and permissible for the players to hide behind a wall, or a stylised row of trees, or, eventually, inside a box. This box was especially successful because of the enclosed echoic acoustics, reminiscent of the original under-stage space of the Trenta performance. The box was painted green to begin with, to represent that *"Invisible Space"* that was associated with the certain empty field or empty meadow where *"the invisible sounds"* had traditionally come from. Later, the stage box of concealment was painted blue to represent the sky, a more neutral and less emotional concept, for the *"Invisible Space"* of the empty field often brought on melancholy or anxiety.

These features, the wall, the row of trees, the green box, and then the blue box, steadily by stages, affected all Gestures Theatre architecture. Stages were now built with a wall running parallel to the auditorium which now ceased to be on three sides and concentrated on one side only. The stage was thus divided into two parts, the seeing and the unseeing, a concept that developed into ideas of high [55] and low, good and bad, past and present. The wall itself, some eight feet high, remained a plain undecorated surface, but increasingly it was made of expensive and highly finished materials, and it was frequently surmounted by a row of ceramic pots, mythological animals and occasionally brightly-coloured plaster birds.

At several theatres in the Wattle, a theatre architect had constructed three sentry-boxes built into the blue wall, one for an effigy of Rowley, one for an actor impersonating The Table Player, and one for a permitted resident Steady-State Player.

69. *Away from areas of innovation, Gestures Drama without vocalisation continued to prosper.*

It became fashionable to attend public performances of massed gestures in synchronisation. Novices paid large sums of money to copy standard gestures in unison on stage. This activity was to be justified as cathartic and consoling by medical practitioners with copious endorsements from the medical faculties who were not slow to capitalise on the phenomenon financially by opening Gestures Drama clinics staffed by elderly or incapacitated gestures performers. When the Marshal of Salutary entered a Gestures Drama clinic at Jundera for a three week training retirement, the medical hospices settled foundation money on no less than fourteen new theatres in the Handy-yard Basin, traditional area of therapeutic baths and springs.

70. *The tensions between non-vocal and vocal Gestures Theatre grew.*

The limitations of the vocalisation of Gestures Theatre being made by performers in hiding, inevitably had to be breached. Starting in the late 'twenties, a history of these tensions leading to greater and greater freedoms can be followed stage by stage. Progress began through the agency of that sometimes neglected Gestures Theatre feature, the dog, a good vehicle for experiment because of its familiarity.

The first strong agent of change concentrated on a form of ventriloquism, with a spate of new performances giving a voice to

[56] what became known as the Rowley Dog. The players making the vocalisations had to remain concealed, but the dog was out in the open, at the front of the stage facing the audience, normally sitting in front of the wall or the line of trees or indeed the stage-box, whether painted green or blue. As was to be expected, the onomatopoeia changed its characteristics away from the sounds of a wounded human of *"the fall and cry"* Trenta beginnings, to that of a familiar hound, and they focused on barking and howling, whining, yapping and growling. And the dog alone on stage created a need for well-trained, patient and responsive canines, a demand largely catered for by kennels in the Grappler district of Housemanstay, where the smell of dog excrement, it was said, made the birds drop out of the sky.

71. Perhaps the second stage of the recorded advance of vocalised Gestures Theatre occurred at Gruton, at a performance of a play called The Happy Hound.
In appreciation of the accomplished polyphonic barking from seven players hidden in a blue box, the applause lasted an hour. Coming out of concealment to receive the enthusiastic clapping, the seven delighted players, as an encore, performed the flagging and waving gestures of the original Rowley at the Rowley cross-roads in celebration of the official origins of Gestures Drama. It now needed a courageous push to make Rowley himself vocal. And that is exactly what happened twelve weeks later.

Just twenty miles from Gruton, at the theatre known as *The Yellow Flag* in Greatingstone, a company introduced a gestures performer impersonating Rowley on stage to accompany the isolated dog. The Rowley player still did not himself vocalise, but he accompanied the hidden vocalising players in the stage blue box with an appropriate gestures vocabulary. He made silent gestures of howling and barking, growling and whining, visually focusing on the dog, a laconic greyhound in this case, with an ironic, baleful glance that held the audience helpless with laughter. The man later fought with the dog for the bones of appreciation thrown onto the stage, the dog knowing that the applause was for him and him alone.

72. Then, on a stage at Kissingrye, the third break-through of great *significance occurred. Rowley finally spoke.*

His first words were a simple identification. "I am Rowley", and, "Rowley, this is me". The words of course were a superfluity, for everyone knew who he was, the Rowley costume identified him, but to have opened his mouth and spoken comprehensible words was an act of revolutionary significance. *"Rowley, this is me",* became a celebrated catchphrase, quoted and shouted, whispered in parliaments, repeated at the dinner-table, at confederation meetings, at conspiracy gatherings, at demonstrations, and, curiously popular, as Irisa Lilkman said, in the bedrooms of temporary lovers, jaded pornographers and couples satisfactorily accustomed to long marriages. It was an affirmation of self, a challenge of *"take it or leave it"*, *"I am what I am, I am who I am"*. A plea for honesty, a demonstration of the common man, an anti-intellectual statement, a statement against pretence, an expression of both pride and humility operating together at the same time. It curiously and suddenly opened the doors very wide to Gestures Drama saying, *"This is a genre for everyone, a place to lay out your credentials without fear, favour or anxiety. If I can do it, so can you. Here I am with my long nose, my pot-belly, my modest unassuming codpiece, my dog, my big feet. I am the man who was nobody, waving the imaginary flag at the Rowley cross-roads, and now you must recognise me for who I am, still no conquering hero, still no wealthy potentate, but certainly me".*

The first performer to be permitted to utter the almost sacred words, *"I am Rowley. Rowley is me"* was Barraud Mopus, a tall man with a swarthy skin from Famadomeer in the South. He appropriately had a long nose, though he was obliged to pad out his trousers to simulate the required pot-belly. He and his dog defined the newly minted role. The dog, a black-eared, white mongrel of terrier-bulldog ancestry called Nipper on account of his predilection to bite the feet of those not wearing clogs, had a predilection to cock his ear on one side as though listening for his

[58] master's voice. Barraud Mopus sometimes spoke the magic words through a speech trumpet to overcome the level of noise created by the excited barking dog and the exuberant cheering audience.

Barraud Mopus was soon to have many imitators. The business associated with presenting and representing Rowley became an industry. Some performers hid their identity within the role and disappeared inside it. Others retained their own identity and wore Rowley like an overcoat. Yet others developed artifices to bridge the gap between. Take, for example, the feature of the padded belly. It was to be called *The Rowley Belly*. Worn inside the trousers and consequently concealed, or worn as a padded cushion outside the trousers fastened to the body with a bold red ribbon so that the audience could clearly see the artifice, the artificial anatomy became celebrated. Pastromo Ostermore identified with it until he was almost nothing else. He wore it upside down, and slipped around to the small of his back, lifted up to his chest and then perched on his head like a hat. It was frequently and obscenely held between his legs as some sort of bum-wiper.

Performers without a long nose adopted a fake one, traditionally to be manufactured in white porcelain, again often ostentatiously attached to the head with a bright red ribbon. Tino Horrase identified with the long nose, pulling it, wiping it, making it sneeze messily, identifying it, of course, with his penis. He even, by a sleight of hand that made middle-aged ladies scream with delight and love him inexorably, made an exchange between the two articles, so that smelling a rose and watering a rose became most peculiarly confused.

A very young actor called Simal Faradale, identified with what at one time had been Rowley's almost invisible mouth. Faradale's act involved Rowley discovering his mouth, a tour de force performance that started with a great blankness beneath the nose, and by stages of facial contortion and grimace, and sudden terrifying swallows that threatened to endanger the nose, the whole face became a jabbering, noisy, all consuming orifice.

The difficulties of acting with a dog were often avoided by stuffing [59] the animal and attaching its stuffed replica to the Rowley costume, sewing it to the coat-tails such that it was always behind the actor, or pushing it unsuccessfully into a pocket, such that it bit the hand of the actor playing Rowley every time he went for his handkerchief. At Goring, an actor playing Rowley killed his dog on stage in a fit of simulated exhibitionist frustration, and ate it, throwing the chewed and gnawed bones into the audience. The following night he was attacked in the empty field opposite the theatre with clubs, and a pack of hungry dogs were set loose on his crippled body.

73. In Beeley, a Rowley impersonator, Hansa Greeta, walked onto the stage naked except for his Rowley props of padded pot-belly, porcelain nose and stuffed dog, all of which were attached to his body by red straps.
His aim was to create hilarity and derision, but also to make a satirical comment which was immediately understood. Rowley had become a fabrication of props. Any original Rowley who might have existed and had sensibility or vulnerability or indeed any character at all, was no longer of interest. Some suggested that this caricature of Rowley, by implication, was a description indeed of Gestures Drama now that it had become vocalised.

The mockery continued, but from both sides of the vocalisation-non-vocalisation divide. If the mouth could now vocalise, what would ever block, choke or stop the diarrheic flow of words, words, words. On the other hand, if vocalisation was to be discouraged, if the mouth was not allowed to vocalise, perhaps the anus could be a substitute. A series of petomanic plays, evergrowing in provocation and subject to heavy censorship, were eventually driven underground into private house performances. Wearing a hip-length, black, rabbit-fur vest that served to make a ring of hair, painting an eye on each buttock, stretching his testicles to make a long chin and ringing his anus with red paint, Waplo Popsilion, bending double, shouted political invective through his anus and made a fortune.

[60] 74. *In a play concerning the simulated murder and dismemberment of a composer to discover his genius, an actor developed a manneristic gesture whereby he turned away from the audience's gaze at moments of high emotional excitement.*

This gesture became such a characteristic that the manager quietly installed a large mirror at the back of the stage so the audience could view the actor's face, for what he expressed was truly remarkable. The trouble was that these high moments of expressive drama only seemed to be possible when the actor paradoxically felt his face was not being observed. For a time the actor seemed to ignore the mirror but gradually he became aware, largely through the excited reactions of the audience, of what was happening, and he had nowhere to turn his face away until he began to hide his head in a shroud which was legitimised by the drama he was playing.

75. *A man scared of time passing, gestured his fears and behaved like the hour hand of a water clock.*

To attempt to allay his anxieties, the man married. His wife became his minute hand, running time-circles around him, regularly crossing his path twenty-four times every day.

76. *An ugly gesture of unutterable grief made in complete silence by the popular actor Friso Herendahl, forced a great many people in an audience at Briderlee on the River Arcuso, to cover their ears with their hands.*

Friso Herendahl became a public hero. He, and the emotional power of his performance, convinced a great many people that vocalisation in Gestures Drama was irrelevant. The event could be construed as a self-evident statement that Silent Gestures Drama could be totally validated. Throughout a long winter of some severity, audience members repeatedly returned to witness his performance. They sat still in the open air, hooded and swathed in blankets for three hours at a time till they looked like a cemetery of snow-covered gravestones, waiting for the finale of Herendahl's performance, when stripped to a loincloth in the blizzard, the huge, naked, vulnerable, ugly man uttered his heart-rending silent cry [61] over the death of a child.

Many who saw this performance believed that the Supremacy of Silence would never seriously be challenged, and the growing enthusiastic swing towards vocalisation in Gestures Drama was seriously questioned in the cities of the Centre Edge.

Then politics and the theatre helped champion silent Gestures Theatre further by a cross-identification. The mauled, burnt and castrated bodies of the Witten Brothers were found on the Dague Gibbet. Conveniently forgetting other political factors, many construed that they were the victims of their own enthusiasm for so aggressively financing Silent Gestures Drama. A shocked public went into a silent scream. The Witten Brothers, who had done so much for silent Gestures Theatre, and Herendahl's celebrated theatrical silent scream of agony became one. Silent Gestures Theatre stood to benefit.

77. Which was truer and more significant, the historical event or its re-creation? Which was believed with more passion and even more sincerity?

There were Silent Gestures Drama performances across the Inner Country that revelled in challenging History which could never be revisited, and therefore could not be wholly proven or disproven. The Gestures Theatre portrayal of history, simplified in structure, issues and dramatisation, became powerful.

What metaphors of history lingered longest in public memory, those portrayed in the history-books or those seen in the theatre? Audiences were learning their history from the activities they witnessed on stage.

The Historians of the Cumber Plain were aghast at the ability of Silent Gesture Drama Theatre Managers to turn thieves into heroes and murderers into saviours. History seemed to many historians to be far too reversible in the interests of entertainment. The murder of a celebrated statesman became an act of righteous mercy, the dangerous conspiracy of a cabal was dissolved into a drinking-shop

[62] joke, the sad death of a philosopher was converted into an event of celebration, a battle of knives became a game of cards, a plague that killed five hundred thousand children became a mild attack of a common cold, an adultery that irrevocably changed the family history of the oligarchy of PastonCumber, became a harmless kiss in the dark between female acquaintances. Wholesale genocide became a quirk of manipulated accountancy. For seven years, it seemed, the metaphors of the Silent Gestures Theatre from the Northern Centre to the Southern 17th Parallel controlled historical memory.

Amongst the many hundreds of theatrical portrayals of history which lived in the memory when the actual events of history had been distorted, falsified or forgotten, was an allegory of Hope performed at Arkansee by Linuino, an ugly seventy year old Gestures Theatres hero persuaded back from retirement. His performance worked on several layers. He enacted a bathing ceremony that related to the history of Agutha, whose humiliations had led to the revenge wars of the East. He enacted a beautiful young weeping woman washing herself slowly in imaginary snow, entirely convincing the audience that the snow was freezing her warm flesh, and that her body, soiled with semen, spittle and urine, was regaining its purity. Audiences were persuaded to believe that a naked wrinkled male septuagenarian was an adolescent female, that the snow was indeed freezing and that they had experienced a convincing allegory of a country renewed after pillage and corruption, whereas the historical truth had seen no recovery, no restitution and no sanguine hope of deliverance.

Historians began to despise the excesses of Gestures Theatre. Where should the celebration of artifice end? To persuade an audience that an naked elderly male was a naked female virgin had a perversity that could not be denied, but should not necessarily be condemned. But to actively pretend that rightful restitution of a political evil was finding resolution when it certainly was not, was not acceptable. Many historians repudiated some of their previous enthusiasms for

Gestures Theatre, and many more began to lobby for reform, and if [63]
reform was not possible, then they declared that prohibition should
seriously be considered.

78. *The writer Ananias Sipperer went to Annatender in the far South-East, and
returned with a philosophy of, not the orthodox dualities, but an innovative
system of trialities that vouchsafed that every phenomenon had three states,
namely, fast and forward, slow and backwards, and neutrality and stop.*
When an audience had been coached to understand and sympathise
with this method of thinking, Sipperer could manipulate their
sensibilities to enviable lengths. Playing the vocabularies of
Gestures Theatre with his philosophies of Triality, he undertook, it
is said, to deceive audiences simultaneously with an imaginary
pursuing cheetah, an imaginary crab and an imaginary block of
salt, and had the audience wounded and bleeding and panting,
damp and scuttling and covered in sand, and choking and dying of
insatiable thirst, all at the same time.

79. *Accreditor, who had amazed audiences with his horse impersonations thirty
years before, and was now working at the Ditcher Theatre at Foy, had grown fat.*
However, his sense of emotional balance and his delicacy of feeling
had not in any way deteriorated. He could still behave with all the
subtle gestures of animal pacificity that had created his reputation.
He fashioned a performance of a docile, modest, middle-aged
woman undressing for the night after a day of unrequited love, who
wiped her vagina with soft paper after a long urination. The
audience subsequently considered why their sensibilities, trained
by practice, prejudice and forced modesty, had not been either
uncomfortable or embarrassed. They came to the conclusion that
Accreditor had so completely identified with the respectable
female he portrayed that they had all felt respectably feminine, and
not at all intruders into her privacy, and second, that they had so
completely subsumed themselves in the act of personal cleanliness
that any sexuality, any feeling of voyeurism, was not an issue.

[64] Nonetheless, two investigating censors arrested the actor for profanity and indecency, even though they had only heard of his performance and had never seen it. They indicated that punishment might well be an amputation of the offending hand. The actor cogently argued that his hand was only obeying what the vagina required for its comfort and well-being, and that the vagina perhaps should be punished. The censors were themselves discomforted, for since the man had no vagina, and he demonstrated that fact to them, how could an imaginary vagina be punished? The consternation of the unimaginative authorities were further humiliated with accusations of prurience. They were caught between what was real and what was imaginary; they could be persecuting the imaginary and ignoring the real. They left the theatre in embarrassment followed by the jeers and laughter of the audience which Accreditor quickly silenced by slapping twenty of the audience faces very hard in as many seconds. The audience-members were shocked and offended, thinking their support for the actor was thus very rudely repudiated. *"On the contrary"*, said the actor, twenty times, rapidly mimicking the twenty shocked and offended faces of his devoted audience.

80. A gesture made by an actor that was no more elaborate than touching the bridge of his nose, and then touching the tops of his ears, and then looking up and into the far distance with a delighted smile.
Did the actor have a cold? Was his hair irritating his ears? Audiences would be very hard put to understand the gesture unless they had been very close to him and had been staring at the pupils of his eyes. They would have noticed the irises of his eyes move as they changed focus, in unison with the gestures of his hands. The man was miming a machine for the sight that had not yet been invented.

81. Because of the introduction of vocalisation, new relationships of vision and sound presented themselves, pushing forward new conceits and ingenuities.

At first there was much play to do with what was called aural and visual asynchronisation, making elaborate use of the non-synchronisation of sound and image that had been established as the first major plank of the vocabulary of vocalisation after the Trenta fell through the trap-door. Variations of orthodox sound imitating the visual, and the orthodox visual imitating sound was endlessly presented, which certainly gathered applause by the accuracy by which one mimicked the other. Then the complexity of this simple language was increased, shifting chronologies, speed and scale. Small gestures were made to imitate big sounds and vice versa, and slow sounds were associated with rapid visuals, and ten ideas in an aural-visual sequence were deliberately put out of sequence, with unexpected grammatical introductions, groupings and listings, even to accentuate punctuation over words. Then, with even more increasing complexity, the grammatical constructions of language, such as rhyming, chiming, alliteration, mesostics and so on, would be put into play, making many unexpected visual and aural connections and disruptions.

Theatres in the South tended to play with cross-language discourses with the resulting enriching of the visual, since the visual can handle more legitimate ambiguities than the spoken, a point not at all lost on anti-vocalisation enthusiasts in Gestures Drama. Word-games were developed such as ironic word-order reversal, and multiple-punning in alternating vision and sound, and virtuoso performances of speaking backwards, leaving out the vowels or the consonants, or simply exploiting one letter, like the initial R for Rowley. Utilising codes for sound that had to be interpreted in visuals became popular, with the word Rowley again used as a mastercode word. The general trend tended to exploit indeed a disassociation of vocalisation and gesture as though it would be too excessive to run them together, as though indeed it would be too much like real life. It was a regular characteristic that one performer made the gesture, another the sound, as though if

[66] one player were to make both sound and image, it would be vulgarly self-indulgent. This characteristic was extended, moving to great complexities that might stretch to as many as twenty, or even more, players. The Fallary Company in Hedeslion in the West deliberately, and very publicly, separated their members into gesturers and speakers, and explored disciplines that steadily drew these two sets of players further and further apart.

And then, almost simultaneously up and down the country, there was a discovery, or at least a re-discovery, of synchronisation which was rapidly exploited with astonishment and joy. Within a short space of time most performers and most audiences settled for the marriage of the visual and the aural with enormous enthusiasm. Many asked themselves how could it have taken so long for Gestures Drama to imitate real life, a question deplored by the Gestures Drama enthusiasts who saw this development as the very antithesis to the whole phenomenon of Gestures Drama.

82. A continual gesture of bending at the waist in a servile way.
This gesture was dismissed by almost everyone, because it was, by almost unanimous public consent, considered too polemical. However, the real reasons were much more complex. First, any acknowledgement of servility was humiliating, both to the servile and those served. It emphasised the inequalities of the community. Then, if society was being mocked and the gesture was ironic, the audience again felt uncomfortable because they knew themselves to be scorned and criticised. Then the gestures could appear to be too arrogant to be endured. Here was an actor apparently, it would seem, acknowledging applause that was not being given, and if not being given, then why not? Then the gesture could be seen to be too self-reflexive, too self-indulgent, and too self-regarding. What was a drama afterall but an event to be applauded and clapped, all the performers deliberately moving towards the finale as closure, making the space before this closure of applause, become an irrelevance, an impediment, something to be got beyond. Why

waste time? Why not move to the applause-ending straight away, which suggested a proposition of some disturbing honesty.

So with critical humiliation, abused community sensibilities, awkward self-indulgences, uncomfortable self-regard, pointed ironies and implied criticism, perhaps the general consensus of the audiences was correct. The performance of a man continually bending at the waist in a servile way was indeed deeply polemical. The performance closed after three nights. In a curious way, the performance had won and the audiences had lost.

83. Suddenly, a series of events that were melodramatic and seemed to be the stuff of fiction, swung a fickle public in a new direction.

First, the reputations of the Witten Brothers, who had been politically sacrificed in such a gruesome manner on the Dague Gibbet, were tarnished by posthumous tales of their masochism at the hands of a paid theatrical mob. Secondly, Friso Herendahl's arrogance, always excessive, but largely forgiven because of his prodigious talent, tipped over when he refused to honour contracts, was cavalier in performance, and flamboyantly advertised his sexual relationship with a mute child. Having been united in a cross-identity of positive support for silent Gestures Theatre, one real, the other acted, the Witten Brothers and Friso Herendahl were united in a sudden negative identity that sucked away support for non-vocal Gestures Drama. Erzo and Hattan Witten's attempt to finance silent Gestures Theatre was now considered to be self-aggrandisement and Friso Herendahl became unemployable.

And then, after such bathos, came the phoenix. Maybe a return to rising exhilaration could not have been possible without the bathos. Fastidio Albignal, the nephew of the one-time notorious Bendeckie Albignal who was responsible for the Trenta fall-and-cry event, saved the popular marshal Leona Leander from a drowning in the Healspont when their sail-boat sank at the Spring Bore Flood. He was made a public hero. This was event number two in the series

[68] of seven fortuitous happenings. Communities suddenly wanted to be associated with Fastidio's enterprises which now included twenty-one theatres, a park and a bank. Fastidio was also very fortunate at that time to have found a potential new Friso Herendahl, a handsome, if plump, young man with delicate features called Porsinio who was exceedingly acrobatic and possessed a novelty - he sang. And he sang in a strong high soprano voice that astonished with its dexterity. Fastidio Albignal also found a new author, Thoma Spendrical, who was witty, satirical and political, and a vigourous and outspoken champion against every new and unpopular PastonCumber legislation. And then, in a performance that astonished and astounded, in the two thousand seater Fastidio Abignal theatre at Arkleek, Porsinio proved to be a woman. Then, marking event number six in this series of seven fortuitous happenings, Thoma Spendrical and Porsinia, as she was now called, publicly fell in love and married. And finally, in item seven in the sequence, Thoma Spendrical and Porsinia were burnt to death in one another's arms, in the great fire at Bakerlighter.

The cities of the Cumber Plain went into a great mourning, and they spent their mourning time in Fastidio Albignal's vocalising Gestures Theatres, listening, more than watching, a series of performances of what were to become the 36 classic works of Vocal Gestures Theatre. Eight of these classics were written by Thoma Spendrical, including *The Sempstress Weeps* where water from tears floods the world, and *The Broom Dance* where domesticity is heightened to heroic symbolic proportions, and *The Woman Reading by the Window* that looked for enlightenment through text. And, perhaps the most famous of all, *A Tower To See the Sea* that brought together all the yearnings of the age.

The two celebrities, Thoma Spendrical and Porsinio/Porsinia, had climbed a mountain and then perished, Fastidio Albignal had become the richest man of his decade, and the Albignal Theatres, had created, almost unaided, the Golden Age of Vocalisation in Gestures Drama.

84. After the death of Thoma Spendrical and Porsinio/Porsinia, and after, [69] *some said, the death of non-vocal Gestures Theatre, a company of five actors consoled themselves and their audiences with gestures of what they called "humour-consolation".*

The activity was composed of slow and then swift somnambulist movements constantly changing in scale, that evoked conventionally recognised good things like love-making, drinking alcohol, babies, seeing the hypothetical sea, building towers, and, a particular fascination for this company, the jumping of small, green, non-poisonous frogs. Commentators could only imagine that the reference might be to a mythical frog called Rowley who in a series of rhyming verses courted a mouse and was eaten by a duck.

The passions, engendered in the public imagination by Thoma Spendrical and Porsinio/Porsinia, were attractive, and political managers, marshals, sheriffs and even ambassadors of the lower and middle ranks began to take an interest in how to turn the Gestures Drama phenomenon to their good advantage.

The Marshal Godbat Federolly, mindful of falling popularity in his parliament, took up a Steady-State Player position on the stage at Cloughton. Dressed expensively, but soberly, as befits a politician seeking respect, he affected an expression of great concentration as he appeared to study the actors. When audiences had become used to him gracing their stage, he began to introduce movement into his Steady-State play acting, slowly moving his head from side to side, combing his hair with his fingers and looking down at his shoes and laughing quietly behind his hand as though to hide his teeth. All these activities he regarded as being elegant and sophisticated, but their subtler meaning escaped those who stared at him and could think that he was no more than deliberately inexpertly imitating the actions of a bashful schoolboy.

Then Federolly began to arrive at the theatre early to welcome the members of the audience with scent and flowers, handshakes and small black pocket-books laced with ribbons in the colours of his

[70] party. And he stayed after the performance to bid elderly audience-members good-bye with ingratiating words of wisdom fashioned to believe that the women were young and beautiful and the men were handsome and intelligent, even when he was talking to the ugly, and to self-evident fools. However, his activities appeared to signify because his popularity ratings increased and he won back some acclaim. Other opposing parliamentarians took note and adopted theatres in a like manner.

The Marshal Laylerol adopted Fayderling, walking up to the theatre gates every evening with torch-carrying attendants, and Abel Kissingor adopted Oystome, hanging flower garlands on the theatre door-posts. The Marshal Volpure and the Sherif Sergeter adopted the theatres of Gwenter and Highseed on alternate nights, both men politically being affiliated to the same *"Muster in the Lake"* Party. The theatre managements acted equivocally, seeing advantage in the publicity and accruing attention, but were mindful of being taken over and losing their credibility. In some instances this happened. The Marshal of Kickering took over the theatre at Balloon and cleared the stage of actors to stage fighting hares, the symbol of his party.

85. The theatres of Billing and Maberlay, once so well supported by enthusiasts for silent Gestures Drama, were now condemned for the self same thing.
Non-vocalising performers were attacked in the street with dead cats tied to poles. "Has the cat got your tongue?" was a popular contemptuous street-cry.

86. Gestures Drama, both silent and vocal, having accumulated so many disaffected parties, began to develop a bitter war with its censors and critics.
These antagonists often repeated the analogy that their efforts to contain the excesses of Gestures Theatre was like trying to put a lid on the sea, whilst the theatres said their fight against censorship was like the struggle of an honest man defending the virginity of his beautiful, virtuous daughter in a whorehouse.

In the middle of this energetically pursued struggle, as always with every combat, was a thriving population of middlemen, fixers, traitors, conspirators, compromisers, dealers, opportunists, spies and under-cover agents. It was a busy fight in both directions towards permanent self-disfigurement. The reactionary censors envied the freedoms of expression wielded by Gestures Drama, that revelled in its popularity, could contain immeasurable metaphors in the ambiguities of the gestures, was not tied down to text to be trapped by laws of slander, and continued to scandalise, provoke, criticise, satirise and sow doubt, to be constantly on guard in fact in a general, but often unfocused, stance of opposition to the status quo.

The centre of censorship was in the hands of the Moderators of the Centre Edge and the Cumber Plain. They were the practical legislators for conformism. And the heart of the opposition was the financial power of the Squearin'al in league with the Gestures Drama Registrar. The historians in between were too busy vociferously arguing and discussing, to be no more than arbitrary and unreliable referees.

When Gestures Drama was wholly silent, the Moderators, prepared to rewrite history, disingenuously declared they had been content to do no more than adjust the colour of the theatre tickets and trim the hero's moustache. Now that Gestures Drama was fully voiced, they were asking for the death penalty for aberrant writers, exile for pernicious managers and life imprisonment for provocative performers. New laws were being drafted that demanded branding for actresses over twelve so that they might be recognised in the street for who they were: a sure sign that the Moderators were losing, and becoming ridiculous, not to say vindictive, revengeful and sadistic.

Amongst their other restrictions, the Moderators, thinking to ingratiate themselves with the Historians by enforcing Gestures Theatre characteristics into legalised commandments, demanded that all performances must have seven intervals, with no interval

[72] being allowed to last longer than seven minutes, or be shorter than seven seconds. Dogs were to be banned on stages of less than 49 square feet. On larger stages every dog had to have a dog-handler and a patch of turf fourteen times its body length on which to exercise. To remonstrate against such absurdities, Manager Blantenou of Phonoptic Park brought a pack of forty-nine dogs into the PastonCumber Legislation chamber.

The commandment that genitals were not to be viewed on stage provoked Allinasaw to issue his audiences with blindfolds with a suggestive directive that peeping was not allowed except in bursts of seven seconds. He provided on stage time-counters telling the audience when to look, and paid them to chant the seconds. A directive that no representation of the renegade Rowley was permitted on stage, said nothing about the appearance of Rowley off-stage. The streets of the major Cumber towns were full of Rowley lookalikes, citizens with padded bellies, fake noses, yellow flags, little yapping dogs and silver strumpets. The last items evolved from a printer's joke with a misplaced S. Some satirical citizens provocatively wore nothing else. The public were excited by this highly theatrical battle and formed factions that squabbled, rioted, fought and bloodied one another. It was agreed that there was more Gestures Drama off the stage than on.

87. The public hullabaloo excited by the Gestures Theatre Dissensions seemed to need grand gestures.
The first grand theatrical fire at Sevenoaks, scale seven, some said, on a measurement of one to ten, flamboyantly heralded in the great days of Gestures Drama. Not till a grand theatre caught fire, it seemed, enabling an even more expensive one to be rebuilt in its place, could its reputation mature.

The Sevenoaks fire started after a midnight Gestures Satirical Drama called *"The Silent Noise"*, a provocative enough title. The fire began under the stage and spread across the auditorium to the dressing-rooms where it trapped a performer in her bath and boiled her alive. It consumed the night's box-office takings. And it fired the seven cork-oak trees that gave the theatre its name. Their burning branches lit up the moonless night, the flaming leaves drifting like fireflies across the open countryside.

Three people were arrested on suspicion of arson. They were an elderly man with a broad-brimmed hat and a clay pipe, a bearded man wearing a cuscorn hat, and a young woman in a night-gown who offered sex to her arresting sheriff in return for access to an open door. These three sounded like characters from the drama on stage. After stooping over a stool for ten minutes whilst the elderly sheriff gathered together his wits and his libido, the young woman ran out into the fields, naked from the waist down, her buttocks a shining beacon in the fire-lit darkness. The bearded cuscorn wearer was considered guilty. Hoping to copy the young woman's escape plan, he too offered sex to his arresting sheriff who declined the invitation but passed the offer on to his wife. This left the elderly man in the broad-brimmed hat, who finally confessed that embers from his clay pipe had started the fire. He had objected to the politics of the drama which he said was agitating for the spread of foreign-language vocalisation in Gestures Drama. He had merely wanted to burn the words, not the building.

Gestures Drama theatres on fire became only too familiar. One December night no less than five theatres on fire made a linked chain of bright lights along the Wary Quarters Basin. Investigation produced a variety of motives, none of which seemed strong enough to indicate concerted conspiracy, or even a regular programme of objection or dissent. It was generally presumed that people thought theatres easy enough targets for arson. Usually full of easily combustible material, they made a good show when burning, especially on a crisp winter's night. In the over-excited atmosphere that Gestures Theatre was now generating, no one seriously challenged their view on the matter. Few were arrested, no one was put on trial, and all suspects were finally released.

[74]

88. Financial institutions continued to invest with ever increasing enthusiasm in Gestures Drama, urging their workforce to become active supporters, not just to watch, but to perform.

They encouraged Gestures Drama Theatre Companies to create popular works that could be produced by amateurs under professional guidance. These companies utilised large choruses or crowd sequences involving as many as two hundred and eighty people performing identically in as perfect synchronisation as they could manage, in the aisles of the auditorium of rehearsal venues, or even in the street outside the theatre with a master-counter shouting the numbered moves in through the window.

89. A newly created censorship board, staffed largely by PastonCumber Moderators made new demands.

They insisted that Gestures Theatres were not to be built near schools, old jousting grounds, cemeteries, flying parks, brothels or gibbets, in order that they should not benefit unfairly from natural community drama locations. The censorship board threatened that if Gestures Drama did not behave with what they described as reasonable responsibility, then draconian legislation would emasculate it. A reply to this threat was a donkey. It was dropped on Antimious Bricker as he walked in the street beneath a theatre balcony in Greatorix. He died of injuries to the throat brought about by the panicking animal.

90. Rowley was honoured in a grand bonfire celebration in Shregger, the traditional political centre for anti-establishment unrest north of PastonCumber.

With a crown of candles, Rowley's plump seated effigy was transported through the city to the field opposite the Albignal Blank-Catch Theatre, accompanied by some ten thousand singing and chanting enthusiasts, all carrying flaming torches. On his behalf, the 5th of November became a Gestures Theatre Memorial day. Commentators were not slow to remark that the dedication was not so auspicious since the 5th of November marked the

traditional day for the burning of the leaves. After the burning of [75]
the leaves, what then – the burning of the fat clown Rowley?

91. A list of potential prohibitions for Gestures Drama Theatre in the North, was fastened to the gates of the Pompoea stage at Kinkildrop with seven iron nails.
The list included no live dogs on stage, no dismemberment of animals on stage, the image of Rowley to be always clothed, no breast-feeding on stage, a complete cessation of pot-bowl urination, no wearing of the cuscorn on stage, no playing of the alba on stage, no naked lights on stage, fourteen seats to be provided for witnesses provided by the Blue Police, and the creation of segregated toilets with a minimum of fourteen cubicles for each sex. And every performance should finish by ten o'clock in winter and by midnight in summer.
By the end of the following month legislation had been passed to make all the above items, apart from the segregated toilets, law. Transgressors would be subject to arrest, trial, physical chastisement, and imprisonment for up to forty-nine days. The segregated toilets issue was unenforceable because of a technicality due to archaic semantic definitions of gender. Jokers suggested that the fourteen seats provided for the Blue Police witnesses should serve a dual purpose. *"If the shits were sitting there already, why waste space elsewhere?"*

92. In the South, Gestures Dramas without sound were regarded as detrimental to the furtherance of the art and were actively discouraged.
It has been said that a consortium of pro-vocalisation Gestures Dramas theatre managers were responsible for this pronouncement and its implications. They were working to eradicate opposition by bribing the city marshals and corrupting the Moderators by the billeting of a Gestures Drama actor on their families, organised after extensive research, to be appropriate to fit in with each family's requirements, be the families scholarly, foreign, exotic, erotic, elderly or with children. It is said that a list was drawn up

[76] to try to accommodate every family need, resulting in an agenda of theatrical archetypes, which may be instructive to suggest how much theatrical ground pro-vocalisation Gestures Theatre thought it had covered. The list included Gestures Drama performers ready to fulfil the roles of Emperor, King, Queen, Prince, Princess, Dictator, Aristocrat, Marshal, Ambassador, Knave, Mother, Father, Grandmother, Grandfather, Step-Mother, Mother-in-law, Wicked Uncle, Virgin, Matron, Wife, Pregnant wife, Mistress, Concubine, Courtesan, Blue-stocking, Whore, Hag, Virago, Widow, Widower, Spinster, Lesbian, Catamite, Pimp, Prude, Pedant, Hypocrite, Witch, Wizard, Magus, Seer, Prophet, Martyr, Holy Man, Apostle, Acolyte, Mystic, Lover, Unrequited Lover, Wit, Scholar, Commentator, Critic, Orator, Scribe, Librarian, Writer, Painter, Illuminator, Poet, Dreamer, Intellectual, Book-Keeper, Time-Watcher, Time-Waster, Banker, Miser, Spendrift, Debtor, Swindler, Adjudicator, Judge, Juryman, Witness, Prosecutor, Prisoner, Jailer, Executioner, Torturer, Policeman, Murderer, Rapist, Thief, Extortionist, Confidence-Trickster, Blackmailer, Stalker, Strangler, Necrophiliac, Pedophile, Pederast, Guard, Fidget, Tramp, Vagrant, Refugee, Refugee's Wife, Foreigner, Traveller, Scout, Explorer, Carter, Farmer, Farmer's Wife, Cook, Gardener, Nurse, Doctor, Quack, Apothecary, Pensioner, Petitioner, Governess, Surgeon, Barber, Melancholic, Choleric, Clerk, Orphan, Teacher, Guest, Host, Innkeeper, Searcher, Finder, Interpreter, Mute, Blindman, Cripple, Flag-Waver, Archivist, Architect, Curator, Menagerie-Keeper, Singer, Dancer, Engineer, Barker, Actor, Clown, Joker, Prompter, Dresser, Giant, Dwarf, Bully, Liar, Soldier, Horseman, General, Herald, Corpse, Ghost, Resurrected Man, and Living Statue.

93. Moderators in the south of the Centre Edge, linking with a group of historians from PastonCumber, and a scholastic community from Wouverain in the Gorenga Hills, attempted to limit word usage in Gestures Drama.
On the one hand, this prohibition was an interesting exercise in literary economy, but on the other, an absurd dictatorial attempt to

take some control of what they had little jurisdiction over. And it smacked of incredulity because what language can ever be governed for long by legislation?

The first of five salient regulations stated that no foreign words were to be used. This created much deliberation of what, first of all, was to be considered the permissible non-foreign language, and then what, in that language, might be considered foreign. One opponent drew up a dictionary list that reduced non-foreign vocabulary to some seventy words in a possible vocabulary of seventy thousand.

The second regulation proposed that all words ending in Y were considered suspect, because, as like it or not, they were diminutives that came from the nursery, and therefore not considered suitable for adult use.

Three, there were to be no neologisms, to which opponents demanded a definition of "new", and asked that all dictionaries be revised to prove any given neologism was indeed a neologism.

Fourth, no word over seven syllables was permitted. This was not so worrying, since it was probable that good synonyms could be found easily, or the seven-syllable word could probably be broken down into acceptable alternatives, though a range of bird names, for example, proved stubborn, their substance being derived from highly refined onomatopoeia relating to complex song.

Fifth, words that referred to bodily fluids, except for the word "blood", were prohibited, which seemed to imply laughably, that the body was a dry vessel, antiseptically uncontaminated by anything a prude could consider objectionable. In certain special medical circumstances it was permitted to use bodily-fluid words if they did not contradict rule three, and the legislators suggested words for these occasions like *eructile* or *eructient, condist, blumes* or *bluming, bellings* or *belliting, jettle* or *jettis* or *ejettictis, yerk, peueckis* and *tiltis* that were so archaic and obscure that no one, not even philological experts in the pay of the Moderators, could exactly pinpoint their meaning. And it was suggested that the Rule Five

[78] legislation indeed itself contravened Rule Three, in a singularly interesting way which was to have created a set of archaic or "old" neologisms, even to have invented a neologism itself in the word demanded to address the case, namely, *"oldlogism"*, (or *"ollogism"*, or even, *"neo-oldogism"*), a most perturbing oxymoron to all those excited about etymology.

The Moderators also put forward a legislative ambition that definitions of time had to be associated with definitions of place, a difficult concept to fathom. Presumably it was again an attempt to gain some control over history related to geography and vice versa.

All these legislative ambitions, taken together proved to be only effective in a very limited way, to be enforceable only in some ten towns in the PastonCumber Basin with ancient names like Wolley, yWhen, Pyres, YuVorst, Parappenawantaneyo, Ouestrecka and Stey. Strictly speaking, examining the niceties of the new legal requirements, the legislature was only legitimately enforceable five hundred years ago, since the legislature itself offended most of the new legislative ambitions, including an excess of "y"s and multi-syllable words.

The five new laws were finally pushed through the legislative system, causing intense puzzlement with the inhabitants of these ancient towns, who, for the most part, were all recent emigrants from the East who spoke versions of Arcanthasan.

94. At Disallow a troupe of Gestures Drama performers from the far South, wearing cuscorn hats, playing the alba and throwing cocineal-dyed sycamore seeds into the audience, introduced a new work called The Gripping Tongue.
The prologue of this tempestuous drama of chin-chucking, scrotum-holding, and refined vocal dexterity centred around the looped consonants of the alphabet. It set in motion a plot that logically could only end in enforced silence. The audience could not anticipate how. Finally the long play drew to a close, and a servant with a snuffer on a long pole began to extinguish the candles. In the

gathering dark, the chief performer on stage called for a volunteer from the audience. The willing spectator was promptly seized as he stepped on to the stage and his tongue was nailed to a board. The audience was appalled. The Blue Theatre-police rushed the stage. The chief performer, known in the subsequent trial as *the Hammerer*, was jailed. The theatre manager was fined and the theatre was closed for twenty-four hours. Notices were pinned up promising heavy fines and imprisonment for all such future offenders. The moaning victim with a bloody mouth proved not to be a true member of the audience but a planted performer, and three days later it was reported that a small boy playing among the theatre seats, had discovered a trick nail, two halves of a metal bolt connected to a springed hinge.

95. Gestures Theatre, subject to excesses of expression, and some said, to excess itself, became the subject of constant appraisal within its own terms and also in terms of general cultural and social affairs.
The ever-expanding familiarity with the habits, contents, concepts, language, grammar, syntax and characteristics of Gestures Drama amongst all sections of the population, also placed it in the special interests of the judiciary and of politics.
It could be said that, despite all the rules and regulations, self-imposed and imposed by legislation, Gestures Theatre was very alive and developing fast, though certainly not always in directions applauded by everyone.
There were three major arenas of concentration; an intellectual Gestures Drama, a burlesque Gestures Drama, stretching from farce to pornography, and a family entertainment Gestures Drama.

The first of these contained great refinements and often had as its subject matter the reworking of historical events based on the premise of *"if only ..."*. It deliberated on reversing or altering historical verdicts like the murder of the heir of Geppram Filo, and the impeaching of the impostor Leastring and the contrived

[80] evidence given at the trial of Marshal Hockinray, and the illegitimacy of Achim Olopper, and the false imprisonment of Panal Cutek. The structure of such dramas was often based on long and complex gestural dissertations. They were viewed by audiences kept deliberately small because of the requirement to be up close to the action to be certain of catching all the subtleties of eye and finger-tip activities. Self-reflexivity was strong and devices to demonstrate artifice were used with wit. There were many aristocrats, ambassadors and marshals as performers, bringing with them, from their social milieu, much play with gloves, long hair, platform shoes, ritualised eating with the left hand, eye-glasses, linen specific to the female anatomy, animal perfume, and at a later stage vocalisation through clenched teeth. They also played much with the colour blue which became essential for facial make-up, such that this type of theatre was often referred to by the critics as "*Blue-Faced-Theatre*", by the cognoscenti as "*Ultramarining*", and by the contemptuous as so much "*Woading*".

The burlesque-to-erotics Gestures Drama often steered on a very narrow ground between acceptability and censored prosecution. It gained much of its publicity and subsequent income from acts calculated to irritate the censor. There was a persistent showing of the buttocks, the least gender-specific anatomical feature, which were often painted red in case anyone missed the point that the buttocks could be beaten. There was much pissing into wooden bowls by standing male performers and sometimes by standing female performers. It was argued, quite cogently, in various obscenity trials that this was satirical comment on the exorbitant fortunes and subsequent arrogant behaviour of the Bantry Conductors whose ammonia industry, needing copious supplies of urine, had a monopoly in the dyeing trade which made them inseparable allies of the great cloth manufacturing industrialists, the Squarean'all Ambassadors. These Ambassadors were easy targets for satire, not least because, as a group, they favoured very

masculine women as wives, women with heavy musculature and
excessive body-hair, and a tendency to go bald on the head at
menopause. These women were by no means trans-sexuals or
homosexuals, but it was forever jokingly said, that Squarean'all men
would only marry women who could urinate standing up like a
gentleman, ideally with one hand, the right hand, guiding the urine
flow, and the other hand, the left hand, twirling the moustache, an
activity referred to for a time, as *"blue soup-pissing"*.

The third area of Gestures Drama was orienteered towards family
entertainment and was characterised by much holding of hands,
cheek kissing, communal eating and dormitory sleeping, and the
wearing of padded clothing which had a sense of anticipating a
perpetual winter that had to be defeated, but might also have been
a very strong reaction to any indications or usages of nudity. There
was also the curious and soon necessary event of the *"Long good-
bye"*. Ten minutes of leave-taking by any character exiting the stage
became essential, and much applauded if it managed to touch the
heart. Commentators said it originated from the very prevalent
anxiety of the plague years when such was the swiftness of a plague
death it was never certain when two family members would ever
see one another again, and a good good-bye was essential.

Outside these three dominant Gestures Drama genres, there were
at various times, other possible subject-agendas, but they did not
prosper well outside local areas. Catchamole describes what he calls
a mystical genre of Gestures Theatre which specialised in after-
dark performances that played on audiences' collective
superstitions and helped to develop artificial lighting technologies
as a by-product.

Another genre was largely based on the theme of the procession as
a metaphor for sequence, chronology and time, and often dealt
with social hierarchies and pecking orders, and the way
communities were structured from emperor to slave. Since the

[82] companies involved were often small, it developed great ingenuities in getting one actor to play many parts in sequence very rapidly, itself a comment on social mutabilities. In some parts of the Eastern Patch, it became very popular such that stage architecture was adapted to better suit its requirements, making the stage shallow but very wide, with many hidden doors so that performers could make quick exits and entrances to change costumes and characters. Sometimes to make a procession appear longer the stage was constructed in two storeys. It was also intellectually fascinated in not giving definitive performances and consequently offered constant variations on its theme, apparently being supportive of one thesis one evening, only to disagree with it the next, making comment on the fickleness of opinion. It was not strong on narrative and only really admired by practitioners within the theatre who demanded forever increasing refinements, and by those addicted to ideas of steady state behaviour, a sort of permanent theatre that never stopped. One procession performance at Nanvivet continued for three days, minutely recreating a society in a state of fashionable change, the product of fifty years reduced to seventy-seven hours, that starting walking slowly along the narrow stage dressed elaborately in red talking in the female language of Grostate, and finished walking dressed in black, talking in the masculine language of Hetrophe, very slowing changing from one state to the other, button by button, shoe-buckle by shoe-buckle, preposition by preposition, adjective by adjective.

96. A Southern Gestures Drama company erected a white canvas tent in an empty green meadow near Bifolding and offered three short plays on the themes of Midwifery, Acupuncture and Barbering.
The Moderator's Blue Police were alerted on account of the company's cuscorn hats and the chin-chucking habit, certain indications, as they saw it, of dissension. Ten officers of the Blue Police made moves to sit on the edge of the stage when a woman

gave milk from her breast to an elderly man dressed as a [83]
philosopher, but they were not prepared for the events of the start
of the third play when the theatre troupe master called for a
volunteer from the audience to urinate in a silver bowl on stage and
have his head barbered. A volunteer duly appeared, and, as he
provided the urine, they swiftly cut off his arm with a curved knife,
throwing the amputated limb into the auditorium. The audience
screamed and shouted and howled. The Blue Police rushed into the
auditorium to recover the arm, but it was not found.

The actor holding the curved knife was jailed for two years and the
theatre was closed for a season. The amputee was later discovered
to be a theatre employee. The severed arm was eventually
discovered covered in flies. Although the facts were kept secret
until after the trial of the theatre manager, the arm was proved to
have been made of wax, and had been smeared with honey. It was
also later reported that the milk came from a cow and the urine was
a very dry white wine. Both milk and wine were drunk to celebrate
a successful deception.

*97. The seven Ambassadors of the Squarean'all, all related for three
generations by blood and marriage, and all in some way financed by the large
fortunes made through the manufacture of cloth, began to see a great value for
themselves in a very public association with Gestures Drama.*

They had begun to invest in celebrating their family solidarity by
mounting large Gestures Drama Events. The most important of
these was their annually sponsored Festival of the Battle of the
Gown, an extravagance that centred on a competitive event which
initially was a grand combat by gesture. For seven years, year by
year, the Festival had grown more luxurious, expensive and of
greater significance in the community life of PastonCumber. There
is no doubt that dress and costume and fashion, so intimately
associated with the event and so obviously giving it its form and
vocabulary, was the major attraction. The Squarean'all Family

[84] collectively knew it was a powerful advertisement for what they represented. However, there certainly were many private and individual reasons why the 200-odd family members were drawn to the Festival of the Gown, and personal explanations for why they tended to give it their patronage.

Ippion Cantoner, for instance, found it a useful way to meet young foreign women from the South who followed Gestures Theatre activities, for he was addicted to their shaved bodies and their sour smell. Yalter, his nephew, inheriting lechery as a Squarean'all inevitability, used the Festival as an opportunity to meet the circumcised boys who traditionally provided catering for travelling Gestures Theatres Companies in the Gorenga Hills. These young men, who sold spiced offal fried on charcoal stokers held in the flat of their blistered palms, identified their trade in bodies and meat, by chewing cartoffle that turned their tongues and lips blue. Zebecca Demuring of the Cartoucher branch of the Cantoner family used the opportunity of the Festival to be allowed to play the Great Alphonsa Keyringer Organ, the proud combined possession of the fourteen Huckler Gestures Theatres. It had four hundred flatbed changes and a peachboard klaxen-peeler. Orangier Muchar found the Festival, with its licenses and freedoms, an opportunity to parade in finery before his grandmother who had always wanted him to prove to her he was a girl. Gregoria Butchery wanted to use the skilled services of the Agrentina masseurs attracted to the Gestures Theatres audiences, and her uncle Jabber profited from the illegal wager-shops that pitched their tents in the shadow of the Gesture Theatre marquees.

These privileged people of the Squarean'all had been assembled annually under the stern eye of Ambassador Holderai who saw it to be his duty to make a united front for family business and family politics. Holderai was an epitome of eccentricity, real and assumed, unconscious and premeditated, easily caricatured. He had one skin-blocked nostril, a product of his birth, and one eye, a product of early youth brawling. And he supposedly had two wives, one aged 65, the other 15, who both, in the Squarean'all tradition had pronounced moustaches. He limped, having one leg shorter than the other, the result of an assassination attempt, and he affected the appearance of a stork by fashioning his clothes to have long sleeves and wide shoulders which he subsequently hung with his chains of office and the stoles and scarves that advertised his profession.

On the occasion of the marriage of Holderai's son, Donalderhyde, to Aspira Septrender, the Squarean'all had exceeded expectations by renting the grand new Fastidio Abignal Theatre Grounds at Acheter for four weeks to site their seventh Festival of the Battle of the Gown. The Acheter complex had five stages, the largest, a semicircular amphitheatre, was capable of holding some three hundred performers and three thousand audience members. The Squarean'all placed several small fortunes into the coffers of the PastonCumber Moderators to make sure they did not have to suffer any interferences. Twenty-one Gestures Theatre Companies took part, each representing their own interests, but also the interests of the Squarean'all, each taking on a mutually decided identity that involved copious costume activity.

The Battle of the Gown, was, in truth, an eliminating competition and like all such competitions, though favourites and likely candidates were sponsored and supported, and there was considerable bribing, rigging, blackmail and downright cheating, the outcome was never absolutely certain, a characteristic that focused a real and true attention, and created allegiances and alliances amongst the entire community of the Centre Edge.

The parameters of the combat had never been so very complex. An elected member of each of the twenty-one Gestures Drama Companies taking part aimed to symbolically strip his elected opponent of his finery, thus enforcing all his vanquished company to follow suit. Seven sets of marks were awarded by seven referees

[86]   as to the categories of Gestures Drama, namely, elegance, etiquette, wit, novelty, orthodoxy, economy and courtesy, and these marks determined what clothes of the vanquished should be removed. Hits, strikes and blows had traditionally been symbolic and expressed through Gestures Theatre vocabulary. Twenty-one umpires, played by dwarfs and children, adroitly marked the strikes with paint on the opponents' costume, using brushes on long poles. Two strikes on a garment forced its removal. All activity was ultimately subservient to the visibly obvious event of the nudity of the vanquished, a condition referred to as being dressed in The Squarean'all Clothes, itself a curious state of affairs, nudity being the very opposite of what the Squarean'all family elected to stand for, but by inference of course nudity was their greatest advertisement. Everyone after all needed to be clothed. Modesty, sexuality, exuberance, self-identity and the climate and weather demanded it.

When the competition first started, it could be said that it was truly an event that was to be considered to be the model for a very full Gesture Theatre vocabulary. All activities were traced and processed through the art of the gesture. But running parallel to the increasing practice in Gestures Drama for mimesis, realism and naturalism, the pure gestures vocabulary was being adulterated, diluted, and overlaid with aspects of physical touch and action. It is true that many of the points awarded according to the older rulings were so often disputed, becoming so much a question of subjective standards, that the combats were often held up for long periods by, at first, polite, but then ever-increasingly violent disputations and arguments, and then by inconclusive physical encounters that left all battered and weary. Audiences became bored. Greater physical combat was easier to adjudicate, more dramatic to witness, less ambiguous to judge and certainly of greater excitement to an impatient audience. So the symbolic gestures were being gradually replaced by body contact and

subsequent disrobing by force. It was still a ruling that blood
should not be shed or spilled, and there were penalties, from loss of
points to disqualification, to control such activity, punishments
punitive enough to make it worthwhile for combatants to fake
blood-loss to disadvantage the opposition.

After five years of such developing activity, it was apparent that
physical contact was to be seriously embraced, and the gestures
referees were becoming no more than symbolic heralds. It was
certainly now a fact that wrestlers were hired to teach the gestures
drama players how to handle body contact, and the costumes
themselves were beginning to be designed differently for the new
circumstances. Tighter fastenings and tougher fabrics were
employed to resist the forced strippings and the rougher grapplings.

Tradition had demanded that each Gestures Drama Company of
twenty-one performers should deck themselves out in exotic
identifying finery and chose a champion to represent them. Each
champion was permitted to wear a maximum of fourteen
individual garments from a strict tabulated selection. First, the
under-linen for torso, waist and hips, buttocks and genitals. Second
the top-linen of a shirt or blouse, and kilt or skirt. Third, the
broadware, being a jacket or tunic, trousers, trews or breeches.
Fourth, the accoutrements, being hat, helmet or headpiece, gloves,
a gown, coat or cloak, shoes, sandals and boots. The choice of
fourteen garments or less to satisfy the clothing list was up to the
competitor or his company, approved by the referees, thus a
combatant might chose to be a lightly-clad attacker and select the
least encumbering garments, or a defender and place his chances of
winning by making his own stripping complicated and difficult.
Combats like this, sparring the quick against the slow, the attacker
against the defender, were the most appreciated by aficionados.

The major Gestures Drama Companies decided upon, after some
years of trial and error, were The Fowlers, Rowley's Ambassadors,
the Watermen, the Butcher Players, the Bakersmen, the Bookmen,

[88] the Games-masters, the Engineers, the Time-keepers, the Lightmen, the Architects and the Colourmen. Not to be outdone, The Blue Police founded a company as did The Historians. The characteristics of the remaining seven companies were kept fluid, and changed every year. At the seventh festival they were the Foreigners, the Artificers, the Gourmets, the President's Men, Floris's Company, the Carpet-beaters, and the Men of the Seventh Leg, a company who, it was ultimately discovered, were determined on a gunpowder destruction of the Squarean'all. Their conspiracy was revealed on the Eve of the Festival. They had placed a drugged Squarean'all daughter with all her body orifices stuffed with gunpowder into the Squarean'all marquee. The men of the Company of the Seventh Leg were arrested and garrotted, whilst wearing, which was, of course, not wearing, The Squarean'all Clothes. It was such a significant event for the Squarean'all Ambassadors, demonstrating their ability to attract and then repel aggression, that many thought the whole drama had been arranged by "the stork" Holderai.

Each champion of each contingent had traditionally been allowed to chose two of seven wooden weapons: hog, pole, bass, suede, trippet, throwl and groomer. Any likelihood that these weapons would be messily and bloodily effective was of course intended by reference to their equivalents in the locations of war, and by inference also to the metaphors of Gestures Theatre, since the archaic words were in origin probably onomatopoeic and could be considered relative to a gesture. At a later stage the weapons were shaped and manufactured from cork-wood and sweet-water sponges, and a hit or strike by such a weapon would be merely a token blow, causing no physical injury, unless the combatants were very unlucky indeed to be hit in the eye or genitals or awkwardly on the temple beside the ear. Now the weapons had become viable again. The trippet, with its hook, could be used to rip a garment from a body, and the throwl, with its noose and its blade, could be usefully employed to pin down an opponent, and slice off his garments. The groomer, shaped like a large comb, could be used to slash and shred an opponent's clothing.

The Festival of the Golden Gown was a seven-day event. Day by successive day at the seventh festival, the drama of the knock-out competition heightened as the failures accumulated quickly. It was a cause of public celebration that the company of the Blue Police departed early, though it was disturbing that their champion appeared to have testicles as big as ostrich eggs. The Historians' champion proved to be a woman and the revelation of her handsome nudity was considered a pleasure that gave their company fifty bonus points.

The outright winners of the Seventh Festival of the Golden Gown were the Engineers, a Vocal Gestures Drama Company from Amadalen who had a reputation for elaborate props, decor and robotics. Their champion was a worthwhile wearer of the long-skirted and glittering Squarean'all Golden Gown, and the Engineers gave a Gestures Drama performance of victory that would amply justify the genre to the general public, to experts, to fastidious aficionados and to foreigners alike. The nonagenarian Historian Edio Confumo wrote a paean of praise. The Ambassador Gustave Pollinger, long-term competitor to the Ambassadors of the Squarean'all, wrote a vicious criticism of the deplorable diminution of Gestures Drama for the sake of reality, which could more easily and profitably be exhibited at the real theatres of war. The Marshal Lucreaux was present to hold up the victor's arm and crown him with a golden wreath, and thus, by inference, to identify himself with the triumph. The Ambassadors of the Squarean'all recouped their expenses, deeply satisfied their advertising ambitions, and performed good business.

As to some of the individual family members, some had gratified their desires, some had not. Ippion Cantoner, seeking his satisfaction

[90] from the shaved young women from the South, seduced two fifteen-year old wives, only to be kidnapped and ransomed by their angry relatives. The Squarean'all were embarrassed, but "the stork" Holderai refused to pay the ransom and his erring grandson lost his ears and the ransom was doubled. Still Holderai refused to pay and Ippion lost his nose, his eyes and his testicles, conceivably devaluing any future possible bargain. Ippion saw no point in buying back a blind and impotent relative, and made it known that he could never be interested, and Ippion lost his head which was impaled on the gate-railings of the Acheter courthouse on the last day of the festival. Holderai dressed Ippion's headless body with an embroidered damask shroud; he was never slow to lose an opportunity to display the family goods. To make certain that the gawking crowds flocked to see Ippion's corpse and take notice of the quality of the burial material that sold at eight crowns a body-length, he exposed Ippion's severed throat and packed it with leeches to keep the blood uncoagulated and dripping into a silver dish. The Marshal Crashlush held the dish for an hour on the Festival's last day, seeking to identify with the Squarean'all, though what part of the Squarean'all effort he wished to demonstrate his identity with, was not particularly clear; was it the Squarean'all morality, brutality, morbid exhibitionism, sadism, sense of theatre, its hypocritical sexual abstinence or indeed its inspired ability at self-advertisement? It was said that Crashlush had suggested to Holderai that he might increase the crowd's voyeuristic morbidity and numbers by exposing Ippion's penis, engine of all the Ippion misfortune, but Holderai was persuaded against such a gesture by Dimi Salatruce who knew from experience that Ippion's organ of reproduction was not so impressive, and could adversely advertise the present Squarean'all present paucity of offspring. Advertising was a sensitive operation.

Ippion's nephew, Yalta, had fallen in love with a coal-heaver's son and had agreed to labour in a Gorenga Peaks mine where he became a universal catamite, dying with a necrosis of the anal canal irritated by coal dust. Zebecca played the Great Alphonsa Keyringer and was commissioned to write an oratorio she called *Rowley Is Singing*. Orangier pleased his grandmother sufficiently to persuade her to afford his surgery to change his sex, but the activity was always a risk, and growing scared halfway through the treatment, Orangier opted for a state of hermaphroditism that he did not regret, and neither did his grandmother. Gregoria married an Agrentina masseur of very pronounced masculine gender, and Jabber was imprisoned for organising illegal wager-shops that had made him so exceedingly wealthy he could afford to buy his release ten times over.

98. A wrapping up gesture meticulously practised a thousand times in rehearsal by carefully folding newly washed and ironed sheets.
The gesture was so perfect that the audience could smell lavender, feel the nap of the cool linen on cheeks, buttocks and calves, and easily see in their mind's eye, a body shrouded, whether for temporary sleep or permanent death was, it was true, not so certain. It was said that the wrapping gesture was prophetic, and indicated that Gestures Theatre, having said all it had needed to say, would be coming to a gentle and positive and confident closure.

99. At Beddowes, at the Taciturn Theatre, the local company, not especially distinguished, but significantly respected to be able to hold two hundred performances a year with full houses, was perhaps the very last to perform traditional non-vocalisation Gestures Drama, eschewing any sound whatsoever, even onomatopoeia.
The resident dog on this occasion was certainly silent. It was a stuffed borzoi whose coat had been bleached white to indicate its innocence at being coerced into human affairs. It swung like a stiff string puppet above the heads of the audience.
A vociferous group of eighty persons had come to force the Taciturn Theatre to close because of its silent performances. A

[92] group who could easily be considered to be the fathers of this present audience, had staged a copy-cat event a generation before, where the desired intent had been exactly the opposite.

A group of seven selected demonstrators sat on the stage perimeter and accompanied all the company's silent stage gestures with what they considered to be appropriate dialogue, singing, foot clogging, onomatopoeia, hand clapping, ululation and barking, the seven vocalisations of post-silence Gestures Drama. They were suggestively called sound-drubbers, or dubbers, a term borrowed for this occasion, from far off in the future (or was it a quotation from out of the distant past) for an art which inconceivably created its vocabulary from projected shadows that were accompanied by sound. The demonstrators were led by the professional agitator, Layash Bricker, the nineteen-year old son of Mitchette Bricker. He had skilfully found profit in the lampooning that suggested he had been fathered by Rowley's effigy at Acheter, thus making him the natural heir to Gestures Drama. It was said that Mitchette Bricker had acted against the grain of her antagonism to the excesses of Gestures Drama, and had crept secretly into the Archeter theatre one night and impaled herself upon Rowley's temporary Spring anatomy, and that she had been surprised by theatre enthusiasts, the theatre elephants, meeting to debate scripts, and had been made to understand that a wooden phallus was a poor substitute for their long noses, euphemism for their longer reproductive organs; elephants are well-equipped to be amorous.

The activities of the Layash Bricker demonstrators was skilful and even amusing, and infected the majority of the audience who proceeded to join in the event as though they might be a chorus. To increase the noise level, subject of their protest, they banged the wooden seats repeatedly on the tiled floor of the auditorium, and splintered the planks of the wooden stage to make drumsticks with which to rap on the uprooted hollow wooden body of the stage Rowley. A lone Gestures Drama performer, a slim and modest young man, clad in a white gown, and certainly braver than his comrades, persisted in his performance, and was pelted with eggs by an angry audience, excited and incensed by the very noise they were creating. He steadfastly continued, his naked and shaven head dripping with egg yolk, until he had finished his act, whereupon he elegantly bowed and retired.

The Marshal Auten was there that evening, seeking publicity. He was aiming to be a candidate for the PastonCumber party opposing Marshal Candla. Supporting a non-vocalisation Gestures Drama Performance, and therefore inevitably handicapped without speech, if he was well aware of his disadvantageous position, any credibility he had gathered to himself was swept away. He left the theatre a furious man, determined on some spectacular revenge.

Vocalisation Gestures Drama at Beddowes had won, classic silent Gestures Drama had lost. But it was a pyrrhic victory. Two nights later, four hundred miles away, not just silent non-vocalisation Gestures Drama Theatre disappeared but all Gestures Drama Theatre disappeared.

100. At An'timenough, seeking preferment and publicity, Marshal Candla sat on a black chair on the stage. He was dressed in crimson silk, his hair was whitened and his finger-nails were polished. A Steady-State Player, Costal Geranio, a young man, plump and happy, sat on the edge of the stage dressed as Rowley wearing a white shirt, blue trousers and yellow wooden shoes. He was accompanied by a small white terrier dog.

The company were new in the theatre. They were strangers from the South. Maybe they had been paid for by the revengeful Marshal Auten. After an hour of performance, all the company members made embracing arm gestures accompanied by noisy chanting, and indicated a desire for a volunteer from the audience to step up onto the stage. At that moment the small white terrier dog gave an appreciative bark, like dogs do. It seemed to be a signal. The eyes of the company and of the audience fell upon the dog's owner, and with

[94] deference and no particular pressure, both suggested that he, the Steady-State Player Costal Geranio, should be the required volunteer. With much bowing and much doffing of their cuscorn hats, and much good-natured smiling, the stage-players offered the volunteer a glass of wine standing on a shallow golden dish, and they requested that he might wish to take off his clothes, that they might reverently shave and paint parts of his body. The plump young man took off his Rowley costume, but kept on his yellow wooden shoes, and continued to hold his yellow flag. The subsequent imagery of the raised knife, the kneeling figure with his shaved head, his blue-painted testicles and red painted buttocks, and the varnished yellow wooden shoes, all caught together in the candle-light, had seemed enigmatic, poetic, erotic, sacred, relevant, dangerous and beautiful.

When the blow fell and the volunteer's head dropped and bounced across the stage, and his blood spouted into the golden dish, there was a moment's pause by the audience to verify whether or not they had truly seen what they had thought they had seen, and whether or not what they thought they had seen was the truth or a representation. The audience remembered afterwards the long wailing scream as the decapitated head rolled, the scream that echoed the first infamous cry of pain at Trenta when Abignal fell through the trapdoor to introduce vocalisation into Gestures Drama. They said afterwards that vocalisation had been ushered in with a scream, and now they could say that vocalisation had been ushered out with a scream. All were convinced that the memorable cry had emanated from the damp dark grass field across from the theatre. Many of the audience turned to look in that direction, finding at last a true but retroactive source for the mystery of "*The Innocent Sound*".

Shouting and bellowing, the blue-gowned Gestures Drama police had rushed onto the stage. There were struggles, arrests, numerous disappearances, a dishevelled Marshal Leisurow amongst them, his [95] reputation, irredeemably tainted by a staged death, was lost. The audience, some said, continued to scream like a sty of frightened pigs. There was a country-wide clamp down. Representation had caught up with reality. Eminently artificial and silent metaphorical Gestures Theatre had succumbed to the introduction of written texts, to onomatopoeia, to vocalisation, to mimesis, and now there was no difference between the representation of the act and the act itself, even in the question of death. Death on stage was the same as death in life. And Rowley had been there at the start in legend, and he had been there at the finish in representation, as both spectator and player. And finally a justification had been found for the stage dog. It had all come to pass.

The Moderators followed up what their Blue Police had started. They had been given what they wanted. Theatres were closed, shuttered and locked. Doors were bricked up. Effigies of Rowley were burnt across the country. In An'timenough, the blood remained unwashed on the wooden floor of the stage, beside a small howling white terrier dog. Leaves and the wind blew across the empty silent space. It was The End of Gestures Drama.

Printed by

POLICROM

Barcelona - Spain

September 2007